3 0132 02120808 2

D0716782

NORTHUMBERLAN ̄ ̄ ̄ ̄ ̄ LIBRARY

You should return this book on or before the last date stamped below unless an extension of the loan period is granted.

Application for renewal may be made by letter or telephone.

Fines at the approved rate will be charged when a book is overdue.

8\12

BELLINGHAM

=4 AUG 2016

1 1 SEP 2012   1 4 NOV 2017
6 MAR 2013   5

1 3 AUG 2013

2 3 APR 2014

1 4 MAY 2014
2 7 MAR 2015
ALLENDALE LIBRARY
DAWSON PLACE
ALLENDALE
HEXHAM
NE47 9PP
6\15

1 4 JUL 2015

Books by Anna Wilson

The Poodle Problem
The Dotty Dalmatian

Puppy Love
Pup Idol
Puppy Power
Puppy Party

Kitten Kaboodle
Kitten Smitten
Kitten Cupid

Monkey Business

The Dotty Dalmatian

Northumberland County Council	
3 0132 02120808 2	
Askews & Holts	Aug-2012
JF	£5.99

Anna Wilson

Illustrated by Clare Elsom

MACMILLAN CHILDREN'S BOOKS

First published 2012 by Macmillan Children's Books
a division of Macmillan Publishers Limited
20 New Wharf Road, London N1 9RR
Basingstoke and Oxford
Associated companies throughout the world
www.panmacmillan.com

ISBN 978-0-330-54528-0

Text copyright © Anna Wilson 2012
Illustrations copyright © Clare Elsom 2012

The right of Anna Wilson and Clare Elsom to be identified as
the author and illustrator of this work has been asserted by them in
accordance with the Copyright, Designs and Patents Act 1988.

All rights reserved. No part of this publication may be
reproduced, stored in or introduced into a retrieval system, or
transmitted, in any form or by any means (electronic, mechanical,
photocopying, recording or otherwise), without the prior written
permission of the publisher. Any person who does any unauthorized
act in relation to this publication may be liable to criminal
prosecution and civil claims for damages.

1 3 5 7 9 8 6 4 2

A CIP catalogue record for this book is available from
the British Library.

Printed and bound by CPI Group (UK) Ltd, Croydon CR0 4YY

This book is sold subject to the condition that it shall not,
by way of trade or otherwise, be lent, resold, hired out,
or otherwise circulated without the publisher's prior consent
in any form of binding or cover other than that in which
it is published and without a similar condition including this
condition being imposed on the subsequent purchaser.

*For Ben Fallon, who wrote a brilliant book report
on* The Poodle Problem. *I hope you like*
The Dotty Dalmatian *just as much.*

The Remindery Bit

Hello, dear reader. I do hope you have been
well since we last met. It is a pleasure to have
your company as we ramble along the streets of
Crumbly-under-Edge once more. We are going to
drop in on Mrs Fudge and her pooch-pampering
parlour again, if that is all right with you.

Now, I do realize that it is possible you are one
of the unfortunate readers who did not have the
pleasure of reading *The Poodle Problem*, which was
all about how Mrs Fudge came to set up her pooch-
pampering parlour. If so, that is a great shame, as
it is a rather lovely story. Also, you will have no
idea what I have been talking about so far, which is
indeed an even greater shame.

But have no fear! I shan't hold it against you. I shall introduce you to all the main characters so that you know who's who and what's what.

If, on the other hand, you are a reader who *has* already read *The Poodle Problem* . . . Well, hip, hip, hooray to you! And because you are obviously a marvellous person with excellent good taste, I am sure you won't mind a quick reminder of the main characters, will you? Good, now that's sorted, let's begin.

This is Pippa Peppercorn. She is ten and a half (she has grown a little since the last story) and because of this she has to go to school. This is obviously extremely irritating, but if you are ten and a half there are certain things that you cannot get out of, and

school is one of these. She would much rather be helping out Mrs Fudge all the time but sadly she can only do this after school, at weekends, and in the holidays. Her parents don't mind, by the way, that she spends all her spare time at Mrs Fudge's place, as her parents are too boring to notice. (As indeed are most parents, I'm sure you'll agree.)

This is Mrs Fudge. As you can tell, she is kindliest lady that ever there was, from the ends of her fluffy white hair to the tips of her shiny black shoes. She used to run a hair salon called Chop 'n' Chat in a back room of her house on Liquorice Drive. Well, she still *does* run a hair salon called Chop 'n' Chat actually (which is where Pippa helps out), but she also very recently branched out into pampering pooches

3

alongside their owners. *And* she bakes, as they say, 'exceedingly good cakes'. All in all, she is a multi-tasker *extraordinaire* and a thoroughly good person to boot.

This is Raphael. He is the postman in Crumbly-under-Edge. He is a great friend of Mrs Fudge and Pippa. He always gets the gossip before anyone else, so he is really rather useful too.

This is Muffles. She is Mrs Fudge's cat. She doesn't do or say much, but she didn't want to be left out.

This is Dash.
Charming! LEAVE ME UNTIL
last – and after the cat!
I ask you . . .
Sighs

Dash is a dashingly handsome miniature dachshund.
That's more like it!

He is also a right
little chatterbox
and suffers
occasionally
from 'small
dog syndrome'.
In other words, he can act a bit big for his boots
sometimes, when actually he is not at all big. Nor
does he wear boots. Oh well, you get my meaning.
He fancies himself as a bit of a detective as well.
(Actually, he just plain fancies himself most of the
time.)

Huh!

However, Mrs Fudge, Pippa and Raphael adore him in spite of (or even because of) his snootiness.

I am beginning to feel a little upset!
Oh, come on. You know we love you . . .

Now, dear reader, I hope that you're ready for what comes next: it's a twisty-turny rollercoaster of a tale with a lot of bumps and bruises along the way, so you'd best buckle up and hold on tight . . .

1

Fully Booked!

Pippa was riffling through the pages of the enormous black ledger next to the shiny red telephone in Mrs Fudge's salon. 'Have you *seen* the list of people you've got booked in today, Mrs Fudge?' she cried. 'How on earth are we going to fit them all in?'

'I don't know, dear,' the old lady sighed, peering over her assistant's shoulder at the scribbled lines of names and appointment times. The pages were so full of hurried pencillings that Mrs Fudge had quite a time of it trying to read what she had written. She squinted through her half-moon spectacles and over the top of them, then she gave them a quick clean on the edge of her favourite blue-and-white

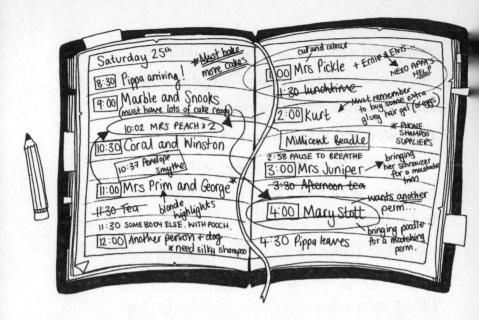

Saturday 25th ✱ Must bake more cakes

8:30 Pippa arriving!

9:00 Marble and Snooks (must have lots of cake ready)

10:02 MRS PEACH × 2

10:30 Coral and Winston

10:37 Penelope Smythe

11:00 Mrs Prim and George ✱

11:30 Tea blonde highlights

11:30 SOMEBODY ELSE. WITH POOCH.

12:00 Another person + dog ✱ need silky shampoo

cut and colour

1:00 Mrs Pickle + Ernie & Elvis — NEED APPA'S HELP

1:30 lunchtime

2:00 Kurt — Must remember to buy some extra gluey hair gel (or eggs)

✱ PHONE SHAMPOO SUPPLIERS

Millicent Beadle

2:58 PAUSE TO BREATHE

3:00 Mrs Juniper — bringing her schnauzer for a moustache trim

3:30 Afternoon tea

4:00 Mary Stott — wants another perm...

4:30 Pippa leaves — bringing poodle for a matching perm.

daisy apron, but the writing remained as messy and undecipherable as ever. One thing was certain, however: there were more customers wanting to come to Chop 'n' Chat than ever before.

Mrs Fudge pushed her spectacles further up her nose and scanned the first page. 'I know it's a lot, but with your helping hand I'll be fine, I'm sure, dear. I just can't bring myself to turn anyone away. Not after . . . well, you know.'

'After what?' said Pippa.

Mrs Fudge sighed. Pippa Peppercorn was good

at many things, but picking up subtle hints was not one of them. 'After Trinity Meddler opened a new salon and took all my customers away,' Mrs Fudge reminded her, rather impatiently.

'Mmm,' Pippa said, her lips pursed. 'That old beeswax. Well, she's gone now. Good riddance to bad rubbish. So I think you could sit back and relax a bit, Mrs Fudge.'

'Oh . . . I know you probably think I'm crazy, filling up my time like this,' Mrs Fudge said anxiously. 'But if people need me, I can't very well say no.'

'You don't think your customers would leave you *again*?' Dash asked, pricking up his glossy, russet ears. 'That horrible Trinity Meddler business was surely a one-off.'

(No, you're not hearing things. Dash can talk. And Mrs Fudge, Pippa and Raphael are the only three people in Crumbly-under-Edge who have the privilege of being able to understand him.)

'I don't think we should even *mention* that

woman's name again!' Pippa blurted out. 'She was a fiend. A traitor! A VILLAIN!' Pippa was shouting now and waving her fists provocatively.

'That will do, Pippa dear,' Mrs Fudge remonstrated (although there was a twinkle in her eye as she said this). 'Why don't you go and put the kettle on? Our first customers will be here shortly.'

'Not before I's had me mornin' cuppa with you, darlin's!' Raphael the postman had appeared in the doorway. He always let himself in. He was part of the family at Chop 'n' Chat, forever popping in and making himself at home.

'Raphael!' cried Pippa, rushing towards him. She began talking at top speed. 'We haven't got time for tea this morning. We're fully booked and rushed off our feet and totally beside ourselves with worry! Maybe you can talk some sense into Mrs Fudge. She's running herself ragged, filling up her appointments diary and—'

'Talkin' o' runnin' ragged,' Raphael interrupted.

'You never guess what I see this mornin'!' He
plonked himself down on a twirly-whirly chair,
propping up his long legs on the work surface in
front of him (which is not very polite, but if you are
Raphael, you can get away with these things).

'No, you're right. We won't guess,' said Dash
curtly. 'So why don't you get on with it and tell
us?'

Mrs Fudge gave him a stern look, but Raphael
laughed. 'He right . . . he won't guess . . .' He
paused until Pippa joined Dash in crying, 'Raphael!
Tell us!'

'Rooaaaaoooow!' agreed Muffles.

'All right, all right!' Raphael said, holding his
hands up to silence his audience. 'I is walkin' down
Liquorice Drive, comin' to see you, Mrs Fudge,
darlin', when I hears a rustlin' and a hustlin' in
the bushes. I looks up from sortin' through me
letters, and I fairly jumps right outta me skin!
A HUMONGOUS dog come a-rushin' out in
front o' me – all white and dotty-spotty it was.

11

I never seen a ting like it in my life.'

Dash growled contemptuously. 'A Dalmatian,' he said.

'A what?' said Pippa and Raphael in unison.

'A Dalmatian,' repeated Dash. 'That's what those large spotty dogs are called.'

Mrs Fudge frowned. 'I know all the dogs and their owners in Crumbly-under-Edge and I'm positive there is no one with a large spotty dog.'

Raphael nodded enthusiastically. 'That is what I is tinkin'.'

'Well, if you ask me, you were seeing things,' said Dash. 'I have to say, I hope you were. We've only just got rid of those infernal poodles,' he added, curling his top lip in a snarl.

While the Crumblies had been under Trinity's spell, she had persuaded them to replace their own dogs with oodles of pernickety poodles. It had been a relief for the canine population of Crumbly-under-Edge when the silly fluffy dogs had disappeared one day along with their wicked

ringleader, and life had returned to normal.

Pippa gave a dry chuckle. 'Yes. Thank goodness they *have* all gone,' she said.

'So was this spotty dog on its own?' Mrs Fudge asked.

'All I seen is the dog,' replied the postie. 'But it runnin' so fast, no human bein' could be runnin' with it!' he cried. 'And I is so shocked,

I is not hangin' around to find out.'

Mrs Fudge shook her head. 'Oh well, I expect whoever owns it will want to bring it in for grooming too. What am I going to do? There are simply not enough hours in the day . . .' She turned her attention back to her messy, overbooked diary. 'I should change the name of the salon to "Chop 'n' *Bark*", the way things are these days. There's certainly not enough time to *chat* to my customers any more . . .'

Pippa was deep in thought, tapping the fingers of her right hand on her chin. 'You know, Mrs Fudge, now that the poodles have gone, you should really have *less* work in the salon, not *more*.'

Mrs Fudge took off her spectacles and rubbed her tired eyes. 'But, Pippa dear, you've forgotten that I have to do the Crumblies' hair as well as pamper their pooches, so I've got double the work I used to have! And I'm not getting any younger, dearies,' she added, looking sorrowfully at her friends.

Quite.

**There was no need
for that.**
Sorry.

Mrs Fudge
frowned as she
ran her eyes
over the page
in front of her
yet again. She
was racking her brains for a way to get through the
appointments. Thank goodness it's a Saturday, she
thought. If I didn't have Pippa's help, I don't know
what I would do.

'So, who's first?' Dash asked, jumping up on to
the sofa and craning his neck. He didn't like to be
left out of anything that was going on.

Muffles bristled and moved along to the far end
of the sofa. She had always considered it *her* sofa,
and she was not terribly keen on sharing.

Mrs Fudge bit her lip and said, 'I'm afraid it's

Marble.' She squinted at her writing. 'Although it could be Coral. I wrote it in such a hurry, and now I can't read it. Oh dear,' she muttered, taking off her specs again and giving them another vigorous rub on her apron.

Pippa rolled her eyes. 'If it's Marble I think I *will* go and put that kettle on.'

Pippa had never forgiven Marble Wainwright for being the first customer to abandon Mrs Fudge in favour of Trinity's new salon. (Not to mention abandoning her perfect pooch Snooks in favour of one of the ghastly poodles.)

Mrs Fudge tutted. 'Marble's seen the error of her ways, you know that.'

'Really?' Pippa said, her face twisted with scepticism. 'I doubt very much that Marble would see the error of anything *she* ever did. She only ever sees other people's faults.' Then, leaving her words hanging in the air like a bad smell, she went to the kitchen to make the tea.

Dash let out a little snort of doggy laughter.

'I don't think you'll manage to persuade Pippa that Marble is anything other than bad news, Mrs F.!'

'Miaow!' said Muffles in agreement.

As Raphael had watched this scene, he began to look distinctly less comfortable at the idea of staying for a cup of tea. Eventually he said, 'Marble is comin' now, you say?' Then he jumped hastily from his chair, sending it spinning wildly. 'Is dat de time? I is runnin' late with de post this mornin'.' He tipped his cap to Mrs Fudge. 'I had better be off. And if I sees the spotty-dotty dog again, I'll keep you posted – cos that's what I do!'

And with that, the long-legged postie was out of the kitchen and out of the door, rollerblading down Liquorice Drive as fast as a greyhound racing home for its dinner.

2

Chaos Is the Order of the Day

Almost immediately after
Raphael had left, the doorbell
rang.

'Dearie me! I'm nowhere
near ready,' muttered Mrs
Fudge as she hobbled down
the hallway to answer the
door.

If she had been anxious
before she opened the door,
she nearly fainted when she
saw how many people and dogs there
were outside, all clamouring for her attention. It
had been bad enough seeing the list of names in

the book; seeing the actual people and dogs on her doorstep was even worse.

Sure enough, Marble was there at the front of the queue with Snooks the Welsh terrier. Coral Jones was jostling for position behind her in the porch, cradling her pug, Winston, in her arms and elbowing Marble quite viciously. Behind them was Mrs Prim with her spaniel, George. And behind *them* was a long line of people waiting for appointments with their dogs as well. The queue

meandered down to the end of Liquorice Drive and all the way out into the main road.

'Oh no,' said Mrs Fudge. 'Oh dearie, dearie me.'

She flinched as Marble and Coral tried to get through the door together, their dogs panting excitedly and straining to free themselves from their owners' grasp.

'One at a time, please,' Mrs Fudge stammered.

'Out of my way,' Marble insisted. 'I am the first customer.'

Mrs Prim stepped forward. 'That's not right,' she insisted. 'Coral and I made our bookings together. And you said we should come first thing – don't you remember, Mrs Fudge?'

'That's right!' Coral agreed. 'Georgie and Winnie *love* having their baths at the same time, don't you, boys?'

George and Winston barked in approval, which unfortunately seemed to set a number of the other dogs off as well.

'Hang on – *I* had an appointment for ten o'clock,'

said Mrs Peach, pushing forward.

'That can't be right! So did I!' cried Penelope Smythe, elbowing Mrs Peach sharply out of the way.

'Er – excuse me, but I did too,' said Millicent Beadle, apologetically shuffling up to the door.

And before Mrs Fudge could stop them, everyone came streaming in, dogs and all, gabbling and chattering as they made their way down the hall; dropping and trampling over coats and hats and scarves and gloves as they filed noisily into the salon.

'How are we going to cope with this lot?' Pippa exclaimed. The room was full to bursting. The windows were steaming up and the cacophony of barking and gossiping was overwhelming.

'I'm so sorry, my dear,' shouted poor Mrs Fudge above the chaos. She was quite pink and flustered. 'It's all my fault. I must have written everything down wrong. I've been so busy this week, darting to answer the phone in between doing people's hair and giving the dogs their treatments too, I can't have been thinking straight.'

'Too right!' Pippa snorted derisively. 'Well, I'm thinking straight, Mrs Fudge, and I'm telling you, we can't deal with all these people and all these dogs!'

'We'll have to,' said Mrs Fudge firmly. 'I am not turning away perfectly good business.'

'I thought we'd been through this,' Dash said gently.

'We are going to give these people what they want and that's that,' said Mrs Fudge. She may have sounded stern, but she was looking very dazed as she surveyed the mayhem; she honestly did not know where to start.

'It's *perishing* out there today, you know,' Marble said, walking right into Mrs Fudge's personal space to make sure she could not be ignored. (Marble Wainwright was not someone who was backward in coming forward, you see.)

Mrs Fudge tried to move away, but only

 22

succeeded in treading on Muffles, who had been attempting a furtive getaway. The poor cat yelped and disappeared out of the door in a blur of grey and white, which unfortunately served only to excite the dogs further.

Marble seemed not to notice any of this, however, so intent was she on getting what she wanted. 'I could do with a cup of tea,' she continued. She blew on her hands and rubbed them together theatrically.

Mrs Fudge gazed out of the window at the

beautiful winter's day. She would not have described it as perishing if *she* had been outside, instead of stuck in a stuffy hair salon, she thought. The sun was low over the marshmallow-coloured cottages of Crumbly-under-Edge, lending them a soft golden sheen; the sky was dusty blue with not a cloud in sight, and the trees and bushes were covered with a spiky hoar frost that lent them the appearance of Christmas decorations. Mrs Fudge found herself wishing fervently that she could walk out, close the door and leave everyone behind.

But Marble had stepped even closer towards the poor little old lady. 'Hot tea,' she insisted. 'With lots of sugar.'

'Of course, Marble dear,' said Mrs Fudge, forcing herself to attend to the matter in hand. 'I've made some blueberry muffins too. That'll warm your cockles,' she added.

'Hmmm,' said the difficult customer, crinkling her mouth dubiously. 'I'm not sure I'm in the right mood for a muffin.'

 24

The barking, yapping, yelping, tail-wagging, gossiping and attention-seeking of both dogs and people had reached an unbearable pitch by now. Pippa saw that Mrs Fudge was stuck with Marble. She glanced at Dash, and Dash glanced at Pippa, and they exchanged a look which clearly said 'We'll have to take control of this!'

The little dachshund took a deep breath and, leaping up on to the counter by the cash register, he addressed the dogs by barking as loud as he had ever barked in his life: 'Everyone, please be quiet and listen to Pippa!'

Pippa also climbed up on to the counter (not a very safe thing to do, but on occasions such as this, necessity comes before safety) and raised her voice for the benefit of the human customers. 'Mrs Fudge will see all of you in turn, but you *must* come out of the salon to give us space to work. Don't worry, I will find somewhere for you all to wait.'

She raised her eyebrows at Dash, who straight away took on the role of rounding up the dogs, taking the livelier ones out into the garden and the older ones into the kitchen, where there were spare dog beds. Meanwhile, Pippa settled as many as she could on the pooch-parlour tables, ready to be groomed, and led some customers out to the kitchen to find refreshments.

But Marble was refusing to cooperate. 'Snooks needs his coat clipped,' she said rudely. 'And he needs it doing *now*. I cannot wait.'

'Be nice if you said "please" just this once,' muttered Pippa, who had returned looking hot and bothered.

'What?' snapped Marble.

Pippa glared at the old trout, her turquoise eyes glittering, and fixing a sour smile on to her lips she said, 'I asked if I should check him for *fleas* just this once?'

Marble snorted. 'I don't think that will be necessary.'

'No flea would dare come near you, Marble,' said Dash, coming back from the kitchen.

 26

Pippa stifled a giggle.

But Marble was oblivious to the cheeky comment: her broad behind was already perched on one of Mrs Fudge's twirly-whirly chairs and she was bullying Mrs Fudge into giving her the exact hairstyle she wanted.

Mrs Fudge listened patiently, and began the mammoth task of cutting and reshaping Marble's bird's nest of a barnet, while the pesky customer moaned about the weather and the price of milk.

And Pippa zipped to and fro between the kitchen and salon, plying the customers with tea and cake in between her pooch-pampering duties. She started work on Snooks, who certainly did need a good old trim. But this was a job she loved, so she didn't mind. (She had always been desperate to get her hands on the hair salon's scissors but had never been allowed. Mrs Fudge had taught her how to use the clippers, as they were safer, and Pippa felt they were the next best thing.)

I do like a bit of snip-snip-snippety snipping!

snip
snip
snip

Even so, it was hard to concentrate, what with the pandemonium around her. There were still far too many people and dogs in the salon having their hair done, their fur clipped and preened and their claws trimmed. (And if you think that's a confusing sentence, it's meant to be: it was a confusing scene.) All that could be seen of Pippa and Dash was a whirling dervish of red fur, red plaits, a feathery tail and skinny arms and legs, all muddled up together in a blur of frenzied action.

Muffles, very sensibly, steered clear of everything, her little grey-and-white face appearing only occasionally around the door with a look of utter disgust on it. Cats do not appreciate any sort of hustle and bustle, and they certainly do not appreciate chaos.

And unfortunately for Mrs Fudge, the morning went from hustly-and-bustly to chaotic to downright catastrophic in a very short space of time.

'Dash, dear, could you pass the clippers for me?'

'What are you doing, Mrs Fudge?' chortled Marble. 'You do realize you're talking to your *dog*!'

Mrs Fudge blushed. 'S-sorry. I'm a little over-stretched today, Marble,' she stammered. 'As you can see . . .'

'Here you are, Mrs Fudge,' Pippa called, zooming over to hand the old lady what she had asked for.

'Hey! What are you doing!' cried Mrs Peach, just in time to prevent Mrs Fudge from using the dog clippers to cut her hair.

'Oh dear, oh dear, oh dear,' muttered poor Mrs Fudge, as she dropped the clippers in her confusion and hit someone's puppy on the nose.

The little dog went berserk, racing through
people's legs and in and out of the furniture,
knocking into the other dogs and banging into
discarded handbags. Dash did not help the situation
by chasing after the poor pup and yelling at it to
'Stop! Stop! You're going to hurt someone!'

Pippa meanwhile had slathered half a bottle of Mrs Fudge's most expensive chamomile shampoo all over the coat of an Afghan hound, and had rubbed at it so vigorously that all that could be seen of the animal was a pair of sad eyes peering out of a mountain of frothy foam.

By this time Dash had just caught a pack of mischievous mutts in the kitchen wolfing down a fresh batch of Mrs Fudge's best apricot flapjacks and was roundly telling them off (which only added to the ear-splitting racket, of course). Then Raphael reappeared.

'Hello, my darlin's!' he shouted above the noise.

The sound of his booming voice was the last straw. All the dogs that had been in the garden came running at the sound of their favourite postie. They charged into the salon, barking, jumping up and whizzing about, setting the twirly-whirly chairs spinning and tying people up in knots with the flexes of hairdryers and tongs.

31

Raphael was on his rollerblades as usual, so he too was sent spinning by the mad flurry of dogs and ended up tripping and landing on his bottom in the middle of the salon, with dogs of all shapes, sizes and colours piling on top of him in a bedraggled, overexcited heap.

'Oh my goodness and heavens to mercy me!' he cried. (Although it was more of a muffled shout than a cry, as his face was covered in dogs.)

'What an al-might-y pa-la-ver!'

Pippa at once set to pulling dogs off the poor postie, and Dash barked orders at the perplexed pups to 'Get in line and behave yourselves!' The dogs seemed as dazed as poor Raphael when he at last emerged from the pile of pooches, and so they did as they were told and meekly went to form a queue in the hall.

'Mrs Fudge!' exclaimed Raphael, once he had picked himself up and dusted himself free of dog hair. 'What in the name o' blazes is you *doin'*, sweetness? You has half de town in here today, by the looks of it. And no one to help you but little Pippa here. I know you said you were busy, but this is crazy, man!'

There was a loud murmuring of agreement from all sides.

Pippa put her hands on her hips and nodded, a thin-lipped expression of disapproval on her pale freckled face. 'You are telling *me* it's crazy!' she said. 'I only wish you could get Mrs Fudge to admit it.

33

She won't turn anyone away!'

'Dears, please don't talk about me as if I was in another room,' said Mrs Fudge wearily. 'I know I've been a bit of an old fool . . .'

Dash rushed to her side. 'You may have been overconfident in thinking you could fit everyone in,' he said gently. 'But you are not an old fool, and I won't hear anyone tell you any different.'

Pippa sighed and let her hands fall to her sides. 'Of course you're not an old fool,' she said. 'But look at this mess, Raphael. You have to agree that Mrs Fudge has bitten off more than she can chew.'

The postie looked around him, nodding sagely. 'I am with you there, Pippa darlin',' he said. 'I tink all you good folk should be goin' home and leavin' poor Mrs Fudge to rest awhile. Pippa and I will be in touch to sort tings out, won't we, girl?'

Pippa agreed. 'Yes, I'll call every one of you

back to rebook, don't worry,' she assured the Crumblies.

And between them, Dash, Raphael and Pippa rounded up the customers and their dogs and ushered everyone out of the door.

3

Raphael's Solution

'You're right of course — all of you,' Mrs Fudge admitted once Chop 'n' Chat was quiet once more. 'I can't cope with another day like that. My bunions are throbbing, and my head is spinning.'

Pippa was slumped at the kitchen table, her head resting on her skinny arms. Her long red hair was frizzled and frazzled, and her body felt like one of the wrung-out dishcloths hanging over the taps in the kitchen sink. Even a ten-and-a-half-year-old cannot keep up for long the level of rushing around that Pippa had done that day.

'I feel as though I have done ten sports days in a row!' she moaned, moving her neck in circles, then letting her head fall back down on to her arms. 'I

haven't even got the energy to go home!' came her muffled voice.

'I have to admit that I am a little weary myself,' yawned Dash, curling up in his basket by the stove. He tucked his feathery tail around his pointy face and was soon fast asleep – and letting out snores that were a sight louder than you would think a dog his size was capable of producing.

Raphael sighed. 'Well, I is not in a hurry to be goin' home. I has been chased all over town by that spotty dog today! I is tellin' you, that is one crazy animal. I don't like it at all.'

Pippa groaned. 'Well, it had better not come anywhere near us,' she said. 'We've got enough dogs to look after as it is.'

'And you still don't know who it belongs to?'
asked Mrs Fudge.

'No,' said Raphael. 'All I knows is, I is safer in
than out at the moment, cos the spotty dog don't
like the postie! Or maybe it like me tooooo much.'
He shuddered. 'Anyway, while I is here, I may as
well be useful.'

And he set to sweeping and tidying and clearing
away the mess the day's work had caused. He
certainly seemed to make light work of it, whizzing
to and fro on his rollerblades.

Mrs Fudge watched him and said to Pippa with a
yawn, 'Wouldn't it be marvellous to have Raphael
help us out every day?'

'Mmmm,' said Pippa sleepily.

'But that's it, my darlin's!' said Raphael suddenly,
slapping the table and making everyone jump.
'That is the solution, right there, starin' us all in de
face.'

'What's that, dear?' said Mrs Fudge shakily.

'You is needin' more than one pair of hands

 38

around here on a full-time basis, right?' said
Raphael.

'Mrs Fudge has got *me* on a full-time basis!'
exclaimed Dash, looking up and putting his head on
one side (which did make him look phenomenally
cute, it has to be said).

Thank you.
You're most
welcome.

Mrs Fudge
couldn't help
smiling at the cheeky charmer. 'I thought you were
asleep!' she teased. 'But you're right, I *have* got you,
Dash, and you're a dear.'

'And what about *me*?' said Pippa, mustering up
enough energy to be indignant.

'You're a dear, too,' agreed Mrs Fudge. 'In fact,
you are absolute gold dust—'

'When she *here*!' interrupted Raphael. 'But, Pippa

darlin', you has to go to school. And do all de other tings ten-and-a-half-year-olds have to do. You don't have enough free time.'

'So – what are you saying?' Pippa asked, an anxious feeling starting in the tips of her toes and creeping up her back and into her hair, making the ends of her long red pigtails crackle nervously.

Muffles reacted to the tension in the room with a plaintive 'Miaow?'

'Don't listen to the feline,' quipped Dash. 'That old furball rarely has anything useful to say.'

'Roooaaaww!' Muffles protested, baring her teeth at the little dog.

'Oh you two, do be quiet,' Mrs Fudge pleaded. 'I have enough to worry about without you fighting like – well, cat and dog.' She looked from Raphael to Pippa and sighed loudly. 'You know, Raphael, I think you've hit the nail on the head. I am going to have to advertise for a full-time assistant.'

'But—!' Pippa leaped to her feet in outrage.

'She's right,' said Dash.

'NO!' Pippa wailed. 'I am Mrs Fudge's assistant and she doesn't need another one. We just have to be a bit more organized with our bookings, that's all.'

'No, that's not all,' Dash began, but he faltered when he saw the flash of steel in Pippa's bright blue eyes and the way she was clenching and unclenching her tiny fists.

'Pippa my darlin',' chipped in Raphael, 'you can see how exhausted Mrs Fudge be.'

'Ahem,' said Mrs Fudge, peering over the top of her spectacles. 'You are doing that thing again – talking about me as though I'm not here.' Raphael and Dash looked shamefaced. Mrs Fudge continued. 'I do think it is worth putting out an advertisement, Pippa. You never know, we might find someone who you will enjoy working with. It could be fun as well as helpful!'

But Pippa did not think there could be anything fun about Mrs Fudge having a full-time assistant. She crossed her skinny arms tightly across her chest

and stuck out her
bottom lip in the most
frightful scowl.

Dash scuttled
over and rubbed his
soft head against
her leg. 'Come
on, Pippa. Why
don't we think of
things to put in an
advertisement? You
are so very good at writing and drawing – I'm sure
you could come up with a brilliant poster.'

Pippa eyed the little dog. 'All right,' she said
reluctantly. (She was a sucker for a compliment.)
'I'll get my pens.' She fetched her bag and pulled
out a pencil case and a notebook.

'Thank you, dear,' said Mrs Fudge, patting her
kindly on the arm.

Pippa sat at the kitchen table and got out some
felt-tips and opened her notebook at a fresh page.

'What do you want to say in this advert then?' she asked grudgingly.

'Hmmm, let me tink a minute.' Raphael began rollerblading up and down while he thought. 'How's about "Full-time assistant wanted to help out at Chop 'n' Chat"? And then we must list the kind of qualities the person needs. To make sure that they are perfect for the job,' he said. He began ticking things off on his fingers: 'Must be punctual—'

'I am punctual,' said Pippa as she wrote it down.

'Must be good with dogs,' added Dash.

'I am good with dogs,' Pippa mumbled as she scribbled away.

'Should have good customer-relation skills,' said Mrs Fudge.

'What does that mean and how do you spell it?' asked Pippa, looking up from the page.

'It mean the person must be good with people too,' Raphael explained.

'But I am *all* these things!' Pippa protested.

'Of course you are. You are tippity-top, mar-vell-ous help – when you are here,' said Raphael, putting a friendly hand on her shoulder. 'But even *you* can't be in two places at once, can you now?'

Pippa puffed out her cheeks and shook her head. 'You're right, Raphael. I know. Let's finish the advertisement then.'

And so they did. And this is what it looked like:

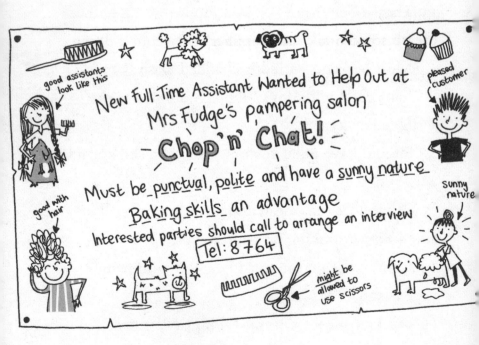

good assistants look like this

New Full-Time Assistant Wanted to Help Out at

Mrs Fudge's pampering salon

pleased customer

- Chop 'n' Chat! -

good with hair

Must be _punctual_, _polite_ and have a _sunny nature_

Baking _skills_ an advantage

Interested parties should call to arrange an interview

Tel: 8764

sunny nature

might be allowed to use scissors

Pippa coloured it in and drew lots of lovely pictures around the edge of dogs being groomed and people having their hair done.

'Well done, Pippa, that is beautiful!' exclaimed Mrs Fudge, giving her a cuddle. 'We'll soon have a string of suitable candidates rushing to our door.' She looked her young friend in the eye and added, 'But I'm sure none of them will be as wonderful as you, dear.'

'They'd better not be,' said Pippa (but under her breath so no one could hear her).

4

An Unlikely Candidate

The advertisement for a new assistant sparked an electric current of gossip through Crumbly-under-Edge, the like of which had not been experienced since Trinity Meddler had arrived in the town. Everywhere Pippa went on her skateboard she heard people talking about the advertisement: parents and teachers jabbered about it in the school yard; people queueing for a bus prattled about it; people in the library whispered about it; even the patients in the doctor's surgery mumbled about it quietly to one another while they waited to be seen.

'Everyone seems to have forgotten that Mrs Fudge already *has* an assistant,' she muttered darkly, as she whizzed through the wet lanes and leaf-

strewn alleys. 'As soon as someone gets this job Mrs Fudge won't want *me* at all.'

But Pippa need not have worried. The first interview turned out to be a disaster. Mrs Fudge had organized it for a Friday afternoon so that Pippa could be there, but when Pippa arrived from school that day, she found her old friend looking rather perplexed.

'I don't quite know what to expect from this candidate,' Mrs Fudge admitted. She was busy making tea and arranging pens and pencils and paper on the kitchen table. 'The voice was so muffled on the

phone, I could hardly make out a word the person was saying, and we got cut off before they could give me their name. Still,' she sighed, 'it's the only call I've had so far, so I had better not judge too hastily.'

However, both Pippa and Mrs Fudge felt their jaws go slack with astonishment when they discovered who the caller was. Surely, thought Pippa, as she gawped at the person on the doorstep, surely *she* hasn't come for an interview?

It was certainly the most unlikely candidate either of them could have imagined.

'M-Marble?' stammered Mrs Fudge, finding her voice. 'I – I don't seem to have a booking for you today, and I'm afraid I can't fit you in just at present because I'm—'

'Interviewing for an assistant,' Marble Wainwright butted in rudely. 'Which is precisely why I am here. And you'd better let me in quickly before I get knocked over by that mad dog that's running around out there.'

Mrs Fudge peered over the shoulder of her potato-faced neighbour. 'Dog, you say? What dog?' There was no sign of a dog in Liquorice Drive.

'Yes, I hope it's not one of your customers'. I can tell you that when I'm your assistant I shall forbid anyone to bring any such raucous beast on to the premises.' Marble pushed her way in, and with a quick glance behind her pulled the door fast with a slam.

Mrs Fudge shrugged at Pippa, then led Marble into the kitchen and offered her a cup of tea and a piece of homemade shortbread. Then she sat down herself and gathered together her pen and clipboard on to which she had clipped sheets of paper covered with interview questions. Meanwhile Marble took three pieces of shortbread and made a huge performance out of munching her way through all of them: crumbs gathered in the corners of her mouth, a thin dribble of saliva worked its way down her hairy chin and she made a lot of rather unappealing noises as she ate. Poor Mrs Fudge had

to wait quite a while before she could start asking
Marble any interview questions.

Pippa was bursting with indignation as she
watched Marble polish off her final slice of
shortbread. Mrs Fudge cannot be so desperate for
help that she would take on *this* old trout as her
assistant, she told herself.

Dash was evidently thinking the same thing as he

trotted over to sit at Pippa's feet, his mouth curled into a faint snarl of disapproval.

Finally, with one last long slurp of her tea, Marble sat back, smacked her lips and said, 'So, what would I have to do as your assistant then? It can't be that hard if *she's* been doing it,' she added, nodding disdainfully in Pippa's direction.

Mrs Fudge was lost for words. She need not have worried though, as Pippa usually had enough words for the two of them, and on this occasion she certainly did not disappoint.

'First of all, Marble,' she said, pouring scorn on every syllable as though she was pouring weedkiller on a particularly stubborn thistle, 'I should remind you that *you* are the one being interviewed, so it is not for you to ask the questions, and second of all, you did not give your name over the phone so Mrs Fudge was not expecting you, and third of all, had she known it was *you* she would have told you where to shove your opinions—'

'Er, thank you, Pippa dear!' Mrs Fudge had found her voice at last.

Pippa snapped her mouth shut and said, 'Fine. I just hope you know what you're doing, Mrs Fudge,' which, admittedly, was quite rude, but I probably would have said the same.

'I think the best way to see if you would be right for the job is to give you a challenge, Marble,' said Mrs Fudge. She winked surreptitiously at Pippa as she said this.

Pippa liked the sound of that and waited eagerly to see what would happen next.

Marble sniffed snootily. 'I don't see why that should be necessary, Semolina.'

Mrs Fudge flinched. She hated her first name. Everyone in Crumbly-under-Edge knew that.

'I would prefer it if you would call me Mrs Fudge. Especially if you are serious about being my assistant,' Mrs Fudge added carefully, discreetly putting a big black cross on her interview sheet against the words 'Be good with people' and

another next to the phrase 'Have a sunny nature'.

'I bet you would, Semolina!' scoffed Marble. 'I should too if I had your silly name!'

Pippa gasped and Dash's hackles went shooting up along his neck.

'You must get rid of this old bat immediately!' he barked.

'And I can't work with that sausage on legs under my feet all the time,' Marble sneered, nodding her head brusquely in Dash's direction. 'He's a Health and Safety hazard if you ask me. Anyone could trip over him, he's so *short*.'

Mrs Fudge hastily invited Marble to follow her
into the salon as Dash gave a warning growl. 'I
think we need to see you in action, dear,' she said to
Marble, handing her a pair of rubber gloves, some
dog shampoo and a set of
brushes. 'Dash here will
be our guinea pig—'

A guinea-Dash-pig

'What are you
talking about?'
Pippa cried,
wrapping her
arms around
the miniature
dachshund. 'First
he gets called a sausage on legs and now you're
going to change him into a different type of animal
entirely!'

Mrs Fudge was shaking her head and laughing.
'It's only an expression, dear. It means that Dash
will be our model.'

Dash looked very coy at this. 'Ah yes, well. I do

have some experience on the catwalk, as it happens.'

Muffles, who had been sleeping on a twirly-whirly chair, pricked up her ears at this and growled softly.

'Not *that* kind of catwalk, you imbecile,' snarled Dash. 'A catwalk in a fashion show!'

'I think this is an excellent idea!' Marble butted in, seizing the shampoo and brushes in one hand and roughly scooping up poor Dash in the other. 'Come here, mutt. Let's see if we can't get you looking half decent for once.'

Mrs Fudge quietly put a big black cross against the words 'Be good with dogs'.

Dash said afterwards that it was the worst twenty minutes of his life. Marble upended the entire contents of the shampoo bottle over his head and proceeded to pummel and push and prod and poke him, all the while telling him he was a 'filthy little hound' and that she had 'never seen the likes of such a messy beast before'.

By the time she had finished with him, Dash looked more like a drowned rat than a dashingly handsome miniature dachshund. His beautiful feathery fur was left sticking to his skin in thick soapy clumps. He sat on one of Mrs Fudge's best fluffy towels, shivering and shaking and looking very sorry for himself indeed.

'Well,' said Mrs Fudge, turning to Pippa, 'how many marks out of ten do you think Marble deserves for her efforts?'

Pippa was bright red in the face. Half of her was furious with Marble for thinking she could walk into the job of assistant, when she obviously had no idea what she was doing, and the other half of her was trying very hard not to laugh at how silly she had made Dash the 'fashion model' look.

'I – er – mfullluggle!' she babbled, hiding her mouth behind her hand.

'Yes, that's what I think too,' said Mrs Fudge. She was doing a very impressive job of keeping a straight face. 'I'm sorry, Marble, but that's a two out of ten from us. Not good enough, I'm afraid.'

'A TWO?' bellowed Marble. 'Well, I'd like to see anyone make that excuse for a dog look presentable.'

Mrs Fudge stood up abruptly and slammed her clipboard down on the table in front of her. 'As I say, I am most *terribly* sorry.' She was taking care to keep her voice low and even. 'But, do you know, I should have thought of this earlier – I don't think I can really have a customer as an assistant, Marble. Think what the others would say! They would think I was giving you preferential treatment.'

Marble bristled. 'But that's the whole point of my coming to work for you,' she said, astonished at Mrs Fudge's evident stupidity. 'I thought you would give your staff reduced rates. I've supported you enough over the years, haven't I?'

Marble, *support* us! thought Pippa. That really took the biscuit. (Not to mention half a plate of shortbread.)

'Thank you for your time, Marble,' Mrs Fudge

said stiffly. 'It was kind of you to think I might need your help. I will let you know how the other interviews go. I have rather a lot of other people to see today,' she fibbed.

'But—' Marble exclaimed.

However, she did not get the opportunity to protest further, as Dash had leaped down from the table and was hurriedly butting her with his very wet and soapy head, which had the desired effect of herding the disagreeable woman out into the hall. Pippa skipped ahead of them to hold the front door open to allow for the quickest exit possible.

Mrs Fudge followed, smiling thinly. 'I'll see you and Snooks soon, Marble. Until then, take care!' She opened the door and handed Marble her coat and tea-cosy hat, giving her a little push in the right direction.

Marble crammed her tea cosy on to her head and spun round, letting out a harrumphing noise as she beetled off down the path.

'Good riddance!' said Dash.

'To very bad and stinky rubbish,' added Pippa, wrinkling her button nose.

'I only wish it was,' said Mrs Fudge. 'But, as you know, it's not that easy to get rid of Marble.'

5

Another Bad Day

The minute Marble left, the phone started ringing.

'I had better answer that in case it's about the advertisement,' said Mrs Fudge. 'Can you finish rinsing Dash, Pippa dear?'

Pippa scowled. She had been planning to answer the phone *herself*.

I could have told them the post was already taken, she thought. By ME!

But one look at the bedraggled little dog at her feet was enough to know he couldn't remain as he was for much longer without catching a chill, so she called for him to follow, and the pair of them scampered into the salon to get on with the job Marble had left unfinished.

'Well, dears!' Mrs Fudge announced, as Dash was being restored to his former self. 'This is a turn-up for the books. Our next candidate is a man! He'll be here in five minutes, so we'd better look shipshape.'

'Why, is he a sailor?' asked Pippa.

'No, dear,' said Mrs Fudge patiently. 'He's a mechanic.'

'Whatever next!' said Dash.

Pippa smiled to herself. He's bound to be useless, she thought.

And from the moment he arrived, it certainly looked as though Pippa was right.

For a start, the man was huge: over six and a half feet tall and with a tummy so round that when he sat down there was no room on his lap for anything else. Sitting or standing, he seemed to fill up all the space in the cosy little kitchen.

He'll scare the customers away! Pippa thought smugly. And I bet he eats far too much cake. Mrs Fudge won't like that.

'Yeah, I've been workin' in the garage for thirty

years. Fancy a change, really,' he was saying, as he slurped the tea Pippa gave him (and took a fistful of flapjacks, she noticed with glee).

If all the candidates are as greedy as Marble and this man, Mrs Fudge will never find anyone suitable! she thought.

'I like your little mutt,' he was saying. 'Wouldn't mind a tiddler like him meself, actually.' He bent down and picked Dash up with one massive meaty

hand, holding him up to his face as though he was thinking of taking a bite out of him as well.

Dash's eyes opened wide in alarm. 'Put me down, you monster!' he yapped. 'You'd better not ask *him* to groom me, Mrs F., or this will be the last you see of me!'

'Ooo, chatty little scoundrel, ain't 'e?' chuckled the man as he set Dash back down with a bump. The dog gratefully scooted under Pippa's chair and stayed there, shivering with fright.

'I – I'd rather you didn't call Dash a "mutt" or a "scoundrel",' said Mrs Fudge. 'I like to treat every dog that comes to Chop 'n' Chat with respect.'

'Ha! Respect! To a little moog like that?' crowed the mechanic.

'Yes,' said Mrs Fudge. 'Respect to ALL my customers.' She let out a small sigh as she put black crosses against the words 'Be good with dogs' and 'Be polite' and went on hurriedly: 'So, erm, what skills *do* you think you have to bring to the post, exactly? I also run a hairdressing business – would

Assistant Must:

Be good with people ☐
Have a sunny nature ☐
Be good with dogs ☒
Be punctual ☐
Be polite ☒

you be able to help
with that?' she
added doubtfully.

'Well . . . I'm
willin' to learn,'
the mechanic
said.

'It's not like
we have much
time to teach you,'
Pippa snapped.

The man suddenly looked desperate. 'Please give
me a shot, Mrs Fudge,' he said, wringing his huge
hands. 'I can't be doin' with workin' in the garage
no longer. There's been some funny goin's on down
there and I don't like it no more.'

Mrs Fudge frowned. 'What on earth do you
mean?'

The mechanic looked around furtively as though
he thought someone might be spying on him.
'Things have gone missin' from me workshop.

Weird things. An old pair o' boots I use for particularly mucky jobs, my favourite overalls – they both disappeared overnight. And then yesterday mornin' I had a lovely sausage-and-bacon sandwich packed up for me by the wife, and that got nicked while I was answerin' the phone! And then there was my towels what I use after I've 'ad to change the oil. Goodness knows why anyone'd want them. Awful dirty they are. But I lost them too – all I could find was a few shredded bits o' fabric out in the yard, like some dreadful beast had torn them up with its teef!' He shuddered as he said this.

'Well, that's most unfortunate,' said Mrs Fudge. 'But I don't quite see why—'

'And then there's the howlin'!' he blurted out. 'Terrible, blood-curdlin' howlin' on these dark winter afternoons. It chills me to the bone! I can't stay workin' down at that garage no more, Mrs Fudge. Take pity on me!'

Pippa snorted and made a big show of clearing

away the tea things and clattering them into the sink.

'I see,' said Mrs Fudge, sighing. 'So what do you think you would be able to help us with?'

'I've got a very useful toolbox,' said the man eagerly. 'Give me a blowtorch and you'll soon see what I can do!'

Mrs Fudge shook her head. 'Oh, no, no, no! What on earth do you think we would use one of those for?'

'We-e-ell,' said the man. 'You could use it to remove unwanted hair!' he suggested.

Mrs Fudge swallowed and quickly changed the subject. 'What about shampooing or fur-clipping or claw-trimming?' she asked. 'Would you be any good at those jobs?'

'I suppose I'd use my pliers and wire-cutters—'

'Absolutely not!' cried Mrs Fudge, slamming down her clipboard.

'But you must need a man about the place – to fix things sometimes, for example?' he pleaded.

Mrs Fudge put a couple more big black crosses on her interview sheet. 'What about my sore feet, tired arms and exhausted brain? Could you fix them, I wonder?' she asked, impatient to get rid of the man.

The mechanic looked down at his huge feet and shook his head sheepishly. 'No,' he said. 'I can't do that.'

Mrs Fudge smiled thinly and asked Pippa to show him out.

Pippa's freckled face was shining with delight as she shut the door on the man. 'That's another "no" then!' she said. 'What a shame.'

A whole week went by and no one suitable presented themselves for the job. Mrs Fudge was as busy as ever and rushed from client to client, getting herself in more and more of a tizz. She gave a spaniel a perm one day instead of his owner and used his anti-flea treatment instead of conditioner on a very fussy lady who threatened to get the salon closed down if Mrs Fudge didn't 'pay compensation' for the 'appalling stench' it left in her hair.

'I don't see what the problem was,' Pippa remarked when Mrs Fudge told her about it after school one day. 'At least she won't get fleas.'

'Oh, Pippa! I can't cope, I really can't!' cried Mrs Fudge in despair. 'There must be someone out there who is reliable enough to take on the job!'

'Hello, darlin's!' Raphael had arrived unnoticed. 'Mercy me, what a mess it is in here. What you been doin', sweetness?' He surveyed the chaotic salon with a frown. 'It look like a herd o' muddy elephants been a-rampagin' through here, man!'

It was true. That afternoon had been particularly trying, and the last customer of the day, a St Bernard, had been the trickiest to deal with. His owner had announced he was in 'desperate need of a good wash and brush-up'. Unfortunately the giant dog did not seem to agree, for he had refused point blank to sit still. Pippa had chased him around the

salon with a bag of extra-large doggy chocs until
she had finally got him into a corner. She had then
leaped on to his back to hold him down while his
owner and Mrs Fudge swiftly tied him to a table leg
with a length of extra-strong rope. Thankfully the
doggy chocs had kept him occupied while he had
his shampoo, but the minute he had been rinsed he
had shaken his thick wet coat all over Pippa, Mrs

Fudge and his owner! As you can no doubt imagine, they had received a most unwelcome shower in the process.

There were now huge muddy doggy paw-prints all over the usually pristine floor, and clumps of dog hair muddled up with wisps of human hair from previous clients. The work surfaces were littered with a mishmash of dog-grooming accessories and hair-care products and there were chaotic towers of used teacups and saucers and cake plates thrown into the muddle.

Raphael surveyed the scene with a lot of tutting and teeth-sucking. 'My, my. I see you has not had any luck with findin' an assistant, darlin'!' he said (rather unnecessarily).

Pippa gave the postie a glare. 'She doesn't need an assistant—'

But Raphael was not listening. 'Cos d'you know who I tink would be de perfect person for de job?' He paused, then threw his arms wide and said, 'ME!'

'What?' chorused Mrs Fudge and Pippa.

'Yours truly! Me, myself and I!' said Raphael, pirouetting on his rollerblades. 'I has always known there be more to life than being a postie. This is my chance to branch out! Go on, Mrs Fudge darlin'. You know you want to give me a go.'

'Raphael wouldn't be any good!' protested Pippa. 'He doesn't know *anything* about pooch pampering. He doesn't even have a dog! And think what a disaster he would be on his rollerblades when the salon is full. He would crash into everything. Besides, he would chitter-chatter to everyone so much, he'd never get anything done. And then there's all the tea he would drink—'

'That's enough, Pippa,' said Mrs Fudge. She looked at Raphael sadly. 'More to the point, Raphael dear, who will be the postman in Crumbly-under-Edge if you come to work here?'

'I was going to mention that too,' muttered Pippa.

Raphael shrugged. 'Someone else will take the job,' he said carelessly.

Mrs Fudge frowned. 'But I thought you loved your job, Raphael?' she said. 'What on earth has come over you?'

'I – er. I just want to help me dear old frien',' said Raphael.

Pippa was shaking her head. 'That's a load of rubbish,' she said fiercely. 'Mrs Fudge is right, you love being a postie. You would hate being shut indoors all day with us. You wouldn't be able to rush around on your rollerblades and you wouldn't be able to listen to your music and you wouldn't—'

'And I wouldn't be chased up and down and roun' and roun' by a horrible spotty dog with snarly teeth and a droopy, loopy tongue neither!' Raphael shouted.

'What?' said Pippa.

Raphael hid his head in his hands and groaned. 'Oh, I know it sound pathetic, but I is tellin' you,

I is scarified o' this dog! Every single time I go out with me post, it leap out o' the shadows at me and knock me flyin'! I has asked every Crumbly I can tink of and no one, nowhere knows to whom this pooch belong. I cannot be the postie any more until someone catch the dog and shut it up.'

'Well,' said Mrs Fudge, folding her hands in her lap decisively. 'I agree something must be done about the dog, but, Raphael, you cannot and will not stop being our postman. I certainly will not have you helping me instead of delivering the mail. What would all the other Crumblies say?'

'I can tell you exactly what they would say,' said Pippa. 'They would say that Mrs Fudge had stolen away their postman and they would be very angry indeed.'

Raphael looked downcast as his dreams of a new job vanished before his eyes.

Dash had been listening carefully. He jumped up and put his little paws on the postman's knees. 'Pippa's right, you know. But don't worry. I will keep an eye out for this dog tomorrow as soon as it's light. I am sure I can follow it and track down its owner.'

'I'm sure you will, Dash,' said Mrs Fudge. 'As for my new assistant . . .' She paused and shook her head. 'It looks like we are back to square one.'

6

A New Arrival

Pippa had gone home and Mrs Fudge was nodding off in her favourite armchair with Muffles snoozing on her lap and Dash curled up at her feet, when the doorbell rang.

'Shall I go and see who it is, Mrs F.?' Dash offered gallantly, and at a nod from his weary old friend he went trotting to the front room to peek out of the window.

Being rather under-tall, shall we say, Dash couldn't just take a sneaky look out of the window as you or I would do. He had to take a running jump at the sofa in the bay window and leap on to the back of it, then soar from that to the window ledge. It was a trick he had got the hang of very early on in his time at the house in Liquorice Drive and he had perfected the art of landing without making the slightest noise, thereby being able to spy on whomever should be at the front door.

In the light of the porch-lamp he saw a young girl with a shock of spiky purple hair. She was dressed from top to toe in black: huge black baggy jumper, very short black skirt and thick black woolly tights on her extremely long legs, and a pair of chunky, clompy black boots on what looked like unfeasibly big feet. Looped around her neck three or four times was a long white woolly scarf with large black dots on it, and over one shoulder she carried a voluminous silver bag. Dash made out the words 'Big Silver Bag' on the side.

How daft, he thought. You might just as well have the words 'Big Black Jumper' printed on your jumper.

The girl's ears, he noticed, were decorated with a line of tiny silver earrings which ran along the curve of her ear and glistened as the light caught them.

She was looking towards the door, waiting for
someone to open it, but as Dash observed her, she
glanced across at the window and spotted Dash
sitting on the sill. She beamed and waved cheerily
as though greeting an old friend, and Dash saw that
she had a small silver hoop through one nostril and
another clamped on to an eyebrow as well.

'Hello!' mouthed the girl.

Dash was startled. Humans did not usually wave and say 'hello' to him. They might smile if they liked the look of him, or pat his head if they were close enough to bend down and touch him. But he had never yet seen a human being wave at him through a window in such an affectionate and, well, *human* way.

I wonder if she's quite right in the head, he thought. She certainly looks rather odd. Maybe she's come for the job.

The stranger was now pointing at the door and shrugging as though to ask if anyone was going to let her in.

Surely she doesn't think *I* can answer the door? Dash thought. She must be one dog biscuit short of a full packet.

He scampered back to the kitchen to tell Mrs Fudge.

'I think you're going to have to see this person. She's not from round here and she seems quite, erm, insistent. And a bit – different from other people,'

he said, unsure how to communicate his misgivings. 'I'm not sure whether she's here for the job or to have her hair cut. It's very odd.'

Mrs Fudge gently removed Muffles from her lap and pushed herself out of her chair. Then she hobbled away, muttering, 'She surely can't be any worse than the people I've seen so far.'

She opened the door a crack to squint at the beaming stranger on the doorstep.

'Hey! Hope I'm not too late,' said the girl, holding out a black-jumpered arm to shake Mrs Fudge enthusiastically by the hand. She was bouncing on her toes as she did so, like an over-excited puppy.

Mrs Fudge had seen some hairstyles in her time, but this girl's was something else. And she's so . . . energetic! she thought. She felt her arm might be pulled out of its socket if she did not stop the stranger from pumping it up and down.

Dash, meanwhile, was sniffing at the air around the stranger as he always did when he first met anyone, person or pooch.

That is an unusual aroma, he was thinking, as he twitched his pointy little nose.

He looked around carefully to see if the stranger had brought a dog with her. (Being, as I have said, somewhat under-tall for a dog, Dash was always cautious in such situations, in case a larger animal bowled him over.)

However, just as he thought he might be getting to the bottom of where the smell was coming from, the girl hunched her shoulders and slipped between Mrs Fudge and the half-opened door. She stepped inside the house, slamming the door shut behind her before Mrs Fudge could speak. 'The name's Minx Polka,' she announced. 'I've come about the assistant thingie.'

Mrs Fudge blinked at Minx. Minx peered at the little old lady, who was looking very confused. 'Unless . . . Oh, no. Have you given it to someone else already?' she asked.

The exhausted Mrs Fudge did not know if she

had the energy to deal with this chirpy, cheery, bizarrely dressed girl. Frankly, she was beyond warming to anyone or anything other than a cup of tea and a hot-water bottle at that moment in time. She stared at the girl for a second and then gestured to Minx to follow her without a word.

Dash was puzzled by Mrs Fudge's behaviour, which he couldn't help feeling was quite unlike his old friend, and so he spoke aloud without thinking: 'Do follow us, Minx. You must excuse Mrs Fudge, she's rather worn out today, I'm afraid.'

'Cool!' said Minx, stopping to scrutinize Dash closely. 'Your little dog's dead polite.'

At this, Mrs Fudge stopped abruptly in her slow painful tracks and turned back. 'I'm – I'm sorry?' she faltered. She was getting more confused by the second. No one but she, Pippa and Raphael had been able to understand Dash since he arrived one stormy night out of nowhere. Could it be that this stranger could understand him too? Was this a sign?

Minx let out a tinkling laugh. 'Only joking. Really chatty though, isn't he? He *sounds* polite – all that cute yappy barking.'

'Cute?!' Dash repeated, appalled. '*Yappy?!*'

Mrs Fudge scooped him up and nuzzled his soft ear against her cheek so that she could

Cute?! YAPPY?!

whisper, 'Shh.' Then looking at Minx she said carefully, 'He certainly is a very friendly dog, I'll give you that. Now, dear, why don't you hang your scarf and bag on one of those pegs there and come into the kitchen.'

'Oh, er, yeah.' Minx hesitated. 'I'll keep my

bag with me, if that's OK.'

Dash watched as Minx hung up her scarf: now
that she was not wearing it, Dash noticed a band of
leather around the girl's neck. It had metal studs in
it.

'Strange necklace,' he muttered aloud. 'Looks a
bit like a collar – for humans.'

Minx turned and
winked at him,
fingering her
necklace as she
did so.

Dash started.
*She does understand
me!*

Big
Silver
Bag

7

The Dog Whisperer

Once Minx was settled at the table with a steaming cup of tea in her hands, Mrs Fudge gathered her strength to focus on her odd-looking visitor. She took her half-moon spectacles off and set them gently on the table. Then, squeezing her tired eyes shut for a second, she pinched the bridge of her nose, smiled, blinked and said to Minx, 'Why don't we start with you telling me a bit about yourself?'

Minx hugged her bag to her, nodded and began. 'So. I'm Minx Polka. I'm from . . . well, I'm not from around here. I've come to the area to do some house-sitting. I've been rushing all over the place, travelling here and there—'

 84

'Travelling?' Mrs Fudge interrupted, suddenly perking up. 'Oh, I used to travel,' she added, with a faraway look in her eyes. 'When dear Mr Fudge was alive, we went all over the world.'

Dash pricked up one ear before collapsing into his basket with a long, doggy sigh. 'Here we go. We're going to hear *those* old stories again, are we?'

Minx laughed. 'Your pooch's heard it all before, has he?' She winked at Dash again.

Dash sat to attention, the fur on his neck raised, his ears pricked and alert. 'She can understand me! I told you, Mrs Fudge!' he said.

Muffles opened one eye and hissed quietly.

Mrs Fudge was so flustered by what Dash was saying that she didn't see Minx reach quietly into her bag, pull out a treat and

slip it to Dash. 'I – er, oh,' she stammered, not knowing what to think. 'Don't pay any attention to Dash's funny little noises. He just, er, needs a walk.'

'I do not!' Dash protested, lying down defensively. He made a show of refusing the treat. 'Don't go putting me out. I want to hear more from this person.'

'I don't think he fancies going out just now,' said Minx, observing Dash closely. Then she turned and caught the look of puzzlement on Mrs Fudge's pale face. She chuckled. 'Think I'm weird, don't you? Talking like I can understand what your dog's saying. Well, I do. Kind of. I mean, not literally of course!' She paused to take a deep breath. 'I've had loads of experience working with dogs. It's the main reason I would love this job,' she explained in a rush.

'Oh?' said Mrs Fudge.

'Yeah. I sort of . . . read their body language. Dogs are expressive that way, y'know? It's not their

 86

barking or whining or anything like that,' Minx explained. 'That kind of thing's important, course. But it's their bodies you need to watch – it's how they communicate with each other, you see.'

'My word!' exclaimed Mrs Fudge. 'How clever you are!'

And what utterly delicious snacks you have! thought Dash. He had not been able to resist the tempting treat for long. In fact, so keen was he to get his paws on another one that he had stopped listening altogether to the conversation going on above his head.

'Not really.' Minx shrugged. 'I learned from this guy I met when I was travelling. He was a dog whisperer.' She put her head on one side and smiled. 'So, about the job?'

'Of course,' said Mrs Fudge happily. At last her problems looked as though they might vanish overnight. 'Have you got experience in dog-grooming?' She tried to keep the excitement out of her voice. I must remain professional, she told herself. This girl could be from anywhere. Oh, I do hope she's not too good to be true!

'Too right I have experience!' cried Minx, her dark eyes shining. 'Dog-walking, dog-grooming, dog-feeding, you name it! I *adore* dogs.'

Muffles's hackles shot up at this.

Minx glanced at the cat, then nervously scratched at her right ear and continued at top speed: 'And I've been bored out of my brains at the moment — I have to get out. This house-sitting thing is total Yawnsville. I mean, once I've cleaned the house and rearranged the kitchen cupboards for the fiftieth time, there's nothing more to do than run around — I mean, sit and twiddle my thumbs. Besides, it doesn't pay that well, and I could do with some cash. When I saw your advertisement, it just seemed perfect. I *need* a job,' she finished, panting slightly.

'Well, you certainly seem enthusiastic,' said

Mrs Fudge, peering at her over the top of her spectacles. 'And do you have a dog yourself?' she asked. 'Because if so, you know you'd be more than welcome to bring—'

'No,' said Minx abruptly. Her cheery demeanour disappeared in an instant; in fact her face looked suddenly quite frosty. Mrs Fudge frowned, and Minx continued hastily, 'No, I really don't have enough time to look after a dog . . . which is really sad, as like I said, I do love them.' She forced a smile back on to her face and scratched her ear again.

'Not enough time?' said Mrs Fudge. 'But, er, I thought you just told me that you didn't have enough to do at the moment. I think you said that house-sitting was, er, "Yawnsville"?' she added, the word sounding foreign coming from her own mouth.

'Yeah, well. Looking after a dog's a full-time business, isn't it? And anyway, like I said, I really need the money. It's not just about keeping busy,'

Minx said. 'So when can I start?'

There was a nagging sensation in the back of Mrs Fudge's mind that she was being pushed about a bit and that she really should ask more questions of this newcomer, but on top of the nagging was an overriding feeling that she wasn't likely to find anyone else as energetic and knowledgeable as Minx.

'All right,' she said slowly. 'Well, it's getting a bit late now and I've had a long day, so how about you come back tomorrow and we'll have a trial run with a couple of the dogs who are coming in for a shampoo? You can do them while I'm dealing with their owners' hair. And we'll see how we go from there?'

Minx's face lit up with joy. She jumped up and rushed to give the unsuspecting Mrs Fudge a huge bear hug. 'Thank you, Mrs Fudge!' she cried. 'I promise you won't regret it.'

'Yes, well – er, thank you, dear,' said Mrs Fudge, straightening her spectacles as she pulled away from the crushing cuddle. 'I am sure I won't.'

And if you bring more of those treats, I won't regret it either! said Dash to himself.

8

Pippa Peppercorn Is Unimpressed

The next day was a Saturday, and Pippa was due
to help out as usual. Dash could hardly wait for
the day to begin; he had been up since first light,
rushing backwards and forwards from the front
door to the kitchen. He was so excited that he had
completely forgotten his promise to Raphael to go
out looking for the big spotty dog.

'When will Minx get here? I hope she won't
be late. I hope she brings those treats again,' he
muttered to himself as he zoomed about.

Pippa Peppercorn arrived bang on time, as usual.
Her weekends at Chop 'n' Chat were the highlight
of her week.

Her voice could be heard ringing merrily down

the hallway, 'Hell-ooo! It's mee-eee!' She slammed the front door, her red plaits bouncing cheerily off her shoulders. She sang to herself as she skipped to the kitchen, her gangly legs going every which way.

'Pippa dear,' Mrs Fudge welcomed her warmly. 'I have some rather exciting news for you.'

She proceeded to tell her young assistant about Minx. 'She is a bit of a wonder, really. She has learned to read dogs' body language – from a "dog whisperer", apparently – and I have to say, she's very convincing.'

Muffles hissed. She was suspicious of anything to do with dogs, and dog whispering sounded very unsettling to her.

'It's true!' chipped in Dash. 'She understood me so well that we thought she was going to be able to talk to me just like you and Mrs Fudge do!'

The more Mrs Fudge and Dash wittered on to one another, the stiffer and more uptight Pippa's stance became. By the time Mrs Fudge announced,

'I do believe she'll spell the end of all our troubles!'
Pippa's arms were crossed so firmly across her
chest that she looked as though she was attempting
to restrain herself from lashing out in fury. Her
crystal-blue eyes were flashing like lightning
bolts; even her hair seemed to crackle with angry
electricity.

It came as quite a shock to Mrs Fudge when
Pippa burst out with the words, 'So you don't need
me any more then – is that it?'

'Pippa!' Mrs Fudge exclaimed, bustling over and
throwing her arms around her small friend. 'That
is not at *all* what this is about! Surely you know
that.'

Dash jumped up to lick Pippa's hand (which was
hanging limply by her side as the rest of her was
crushed into Mrs Fudge's large cuddly frame). 'Mrs
Fudge is only relieved to have found someone to
help,' he said, in an effort to console his friend.
'And when you meet Minx, I'm sure you'll like
her too!'

Pippa shrugged off Mrs Fudge's warm embrace and scowled at the pair of well-meaning faces in front of her. 'Well, I'm very upset,' she said. 'I am the only assistant round here and I don't want some know-it-all person who whispers to dogs taking over from me. So there.'

'Miaow,' Muffles mewed in agreement.

'Now, now,' said Mrs Fudge consolingly. 'No one is going to be "taking over" from you. Sit down and have a cup of hot chocolate and we'll talk about this properly.'

After a good fifteen minutes of gentle persuasion and a second cup of steaming, creamy hot chocolate, Pippa grudgingly agreed that she would give Minx a chance.

'I am *so* pleased,' said Mrs Fudge with feeling.

Pippa grimaced. She could not quite manage
a smile.

The doorbell rang as Pippa was washing up the
cups. 'I'll get it, shall I?' she offered. She didn't wait
for an answer, whizzing down the hallway before
Mrs Fudge had a chance to take off her apron.

I have to get a moment to myself with this person
so I can make up my mind without anyone trying
to persuade me that I *should* like her, she thought.

She had become super-steamy hot under the
collar of her polo-neck jumper, so when she
unlatched the door she opened it a little too
violently in a rush to let in some fresh air. As the
door flew open, lots of things happened at once:
Pippa lost her balance, pitching forward on one foot
and flailing wildly with one arm, and as she tried
to keep herself upright by holding on to the door
with her other hand, a large spotty animal (freakily
spotty, Pippa thought) shot past the house and
disappeared into the bushes outside.

Before Pippa could cry out, or decide whether
to run after the dog, a very dishevelled, extremely
strange-looking girl emerged from the bushes.
She looked around wildly as she raked her hands
through her hair and brushed herself down.

'Whhhooooa!' said Pippa, spitting out one of her
plaits which had got lodged in between her teeth in
the confusion. 'Did you see that dog?'

'Yeah, crazy!' cried the girl cheerily, scratching at
her ear before again running her hands through her
spiky hair (which was blue that morning). 'It nearly

knocked me over. I'm Minx.' She bounded over, grabbed Pippa's hand and began pumping it up and down as she had done to Mrs Fudge the day before. 'I'm Mrs Fudge's new assistant. Who are you?'

Pippa's face clouded over. How dare this person confidently describe herself as 'Mrs Fudge's new assistant'? Mrs Fudge had said she was only on trial for now!

'I'm Pippa,' she muttered, dropping Minx's hand. She turned on her heel, leaving the girl on the doorstep.

'Well, hey, "I'm Pippa"!' Minx called, stepping into the house. 'Nice to meet you!'

And it certainly is NOT nice to meet you, Pippa chuntered to herself crossly as she stomped into the kitchen. Who does she think she is, laughing at me and taking the mickey out of my name? And what kind of weird loo brush is that on her head?

She had reached the kitchen, and was glaring at Dash and Mrs Fudge. 'That new person is here. You didn't tell me she had blue hair and freaky clothes and a head full of metal,' she said.

Oh dear, thought Dash.

'Ah,' said Mrs Fudge.

'Miaaaaaow?' growled Muffles, which roughly translates as 'Whatever next?' The poor cat was wondering if she would be allowed five minutes' peace in her own house ever again.

99

'Hey, Mrs F.!' called Minx, coming in behind Pippa. 'Thought I'd change my look for my first day. Like it?'

'Er, lovely,' Mrs Fudge said, squinting uneasily at Minx's hair. 'You evidently know, er, a little about hairdressing.' (Mrs Fudge was not keen on wild hairstyles. She of course gave her customers whatever they wanted and had done a superb Mohican on a Crumbly called Kurt when he had asked for one. But as a rule she liked the more traditional approach to hairdressing.) 'And you're just in time, Minx,' Mrs Fudge went on. 'Pippa, you should give her a quick tour before Mrs Prim's appointment.'

'Cool! I've brought some biscuits for the dogs. Hope you don't mind? Your advertisement said "baking skills an advantage", so I made these myself.' Minx reached into her Big Silver Bag and brought out a plastic container, rattling it merrily.

Dash stared at the box longingly, his tongue hanging out.

Pippa grimaced. ' "I baked these myself,"' she mimicked in a quiet sing-songy voice.

'Pippa,' said Mrs Fudge, giving her a warning look over the top of her half-moon spectacles, 'would you like to take Minx's bag and hang it up?'

'It's fine,' said Minx quickly. She hugged her Big Silver Bag closely to her. 'Thanks, though,' she added.

Pippa shrugged and led Minx into the salon. As if I care what she does with her stupid bag, she thought.

Dash padded behind the girls, keeping a beady eye on Minx's bag in case she should let one of her treats slip out. He sniffed at the air, vaguely thinking that he might try to discover a bit more about the stranger.

His first impressions had been nothing but good, but the loyal little dog still felt he owed it to Mrs Fudge to find out as much as he could. After all, the last newcomer to Crumbly-under-Edge had been Trinity Meddler, and she had certainly not been good news.

Strange, he thought, as he snuffled at her feet. She doesn't smell like she did yesterday. In fact, there's another smell on top of the original one . . . I think I can detect a nasty niff of . . . rotten vegetables?

But just as Dash was having this thought, Minx *did* drop a treat, right in front of his nose! He gobbled it up straight away and was soon in a happy daydream again while Minx kept up a steady, friendly stream of chatter to Pippa.

Pippa, on the other hand, was finding it hard to think kind and welcoming thoughts. I am going to

ask Dash to help me keep a very close eye on her, she thought darkly. The slightest whiff of trouble, and I'll make sure she's out on that ridiculously over-pierced ear of hers.

9

Minx Charms the Crumblies

Mrs Prim was flustered and out of breath when she arrived for her appointment: her springer spaniel, George, was tying himself into knots as he wound his lead round and round her legs until they resembled the bottom half of an Egyptian mummy.

'Oh my goodness!' cried Pippa. 'Here, let me help.' She lunged at the lead and grasped it with both hands. Once she was sure she had a firm grip she pulled sharply, and Mrs Prim was sent spinning down the hall, freed, but decidedly dizzy.

'Pippa, you are a treasure,' gasped Mrs Prim, as she waited for her head to stop whirring. 'This pooch of mine has been a very naughty boy this morning. Very naughty indeed!' she exclaimed,

 104

aiming her comments at George, who did not seem to realize he was being told off. On the contrary, he was wagging his tail and panting excitedly. 'We went for our usual walk in the park,' went on Mrs Prim, 'and there was a *huge* spotty dog running riot – goodness knows whose it is; I can't say I've seen it around before. In any case, George went tearing after it, thinking no doubt that he could play a lovely game of chase. He *would* not come back when I called and so I had to run after him, and by the time I'd caught up with him the dog had gone. Oh! I'm exhausted! I didn't think I was going to get him back in time for our appointment!'

'Hmm,' said Pippa, holding tightly on to George's lead. 'A spotty dog, you say? You know, I think I saw it too – out the front here – just before our new assis— Oh, George, stop it!' she broke off to reprimand the spaniel, who was certainly very springy today.

'I don't know, dear,' said Mrs Prim. 'But whoever owns it has got a right handful there, that's all I'm saying.'

'And Raphael has seen it too, you know—' Pippa began again, but she was cut short once again by George, who barked very loudly, his tail wagging, his tongue hanging out of a smiling mouth.

Pippa observed this with interest. She could have sworn that George was trying to tell Mrs Prim something. Such a shame that I can't understand

every dog the same way I can Dash, she thought to herself. Maybe George knows where the spotty dog has come from?

She was about to say as much when George wrenched himself free of her control and made for the door. Pippa gave it a swift click to ensure it was firmly closed and then dived for the spaniel to prevent him from bolting again.

He sat down firmly on the doormat and began barking and barking as though he was convinced he could break the door down with the racket he was making. If Pippa didn't know better she could have sworn he was saying something along the lines of 'Let me outta here! I've got places to go, spotty pooches to see.'

The commotion brought Minx running from the salon where she had been helping Mrs Fudge get organized.

'What's up?' Minx was asking. 'Boy! What a noise! Hello,' she said in the same breath, turning to Mrs Prim and grinning. 'I'm Minx. And you must be Mrs Prim. And you –' she paused to fix her attention wholeheartedly on the dog. Her eyes widened and her nose wrinkled as if sniffing at the most exquisite rose. When she spoke again her voice had dropped to a much slower, calmer velvety croon. 'You gorgeous thing! You must be George.'

The effect of Minx's voice on George was instantaneous. His eyes were on the new assistant as if he was entranced. He looked as though he thought Minx to be the most captivating creature he had ever seen: he was sitting bolt upright in a perfectly attentive position, his tail wagging very gently, his face soft and expectant. (Even Pippa had to admit that one good thing had come of this: George's frantic barking was a thing

of the past.) Minx gave him a gentle pat on the head and slipped a biscuit into his mouth. 'Good boy!' she said.

Pippa too was silenced by this strange performance (although, if you had asked her about it later, she would have argued that the only reason she was quiet was because she was watching Minx *very carefully* to see what she was up to).

Finally Mrs Prim stammered, 'M-my, I – I can see why Mrs Fudge has employed you, young lady. You certainly have quite an effect on Georgie. I could have done with your help in the park this morning.'

'The park?' Minx asked.

'Yes, Mrs Prim was just saying she had seen a spotty dog causing chaos in the park,' Pippa said, glaring at Minx pointedly. 'And it reminded me that I had seen it too. Just before you arrived, actually.' She was beginning to wonder if Minx and the dog were actually connected in some way.

'Mmm?' said Minx, scratching her ear.

109

'Yes, it was such a to-do,' said Mrs Prim, and retold her tale of stress and woe. 'A huge dog, it was — one we've never seen before. White with black splodges, a Dalmatian, I think. Utter nightmare — who *knows* where the owner is!'

Minx had turned away abruptly. 'I'm — I'm sorry to hear that,' she said.

'It's all right, dear,' said Mrs Prim. 'No harm done, as it happens. I'm only a little out of puff.'

Minx gave Mrs Prim a careful look over her shoulder, then as if someone had flicked a switch, she beamed and said brightly, 'OK, that's cool. Follow me!'

Pippa had watched this exchange with keen interest.

I must tell Dash, she thought as she went through to the salon.

Much to Pippa's annoyance, Minx's charm and expertise had the effect of winning over every single one of Mrs Fudge's customers that day. At one

point in the afternoon there was a scary moment
when an Alsatian that had come in to have his claws
clipped had terrified two small terriers who were
waiting to be bathed.

'It's all right, you
two,' Minx
told them, as
they quivered
on their leads
in front of
the huge,
slathering
beast baring his teeth at them. 'He's cool, he only
looks fierce.' And she put her hand gently on the
Alsatian's neck and stroked him as if to show he
wouldn't hurt a fly.

Then she led the shivering terriers over to let
the Alsatian have an inquisitive sniff. Once all the
dogs were calm, Minx rewarded them with some of
her treats and within seconds the three dogs were
scurrying around each other, tails wagging happily.

'How did you get them to make friends like that?' Mrs Fudge asked, in awe.

'Amazing,' agreed the dogs' owners.

Minx looked bashful. ''S just that sometimes different breeds don't read each other right,' she said. 'Like – even humans think Alsatians look rough, don't they?'

Mrs Fudge nodded.

'You know why? It's only cos their ears are always pointy, their tails are always up and their eyes have a sharp, alert look about them. It sends out this signal that they are aggressive.'

Pippa was sceptical. 'How?'

'Well, to dogs, if another dog has pointy ears, it means "I'm the top dog". It's all down to how dogs would behave if they were still in packs – in the wild, I mean,' Minx explained.

'She's right,' Dash said, sidling up to Pippa and sitting quietly at her feet.

Pippa scowled. She made sure Minx was busy with customers and beckoned to Dash to

 112

follow her out to the kitchen.

'Listen,' she said. 'I think there's something really weird about Minx.'

'Oh, Pippa,' said Dash sadly. 'You can't say that after everything she's done today! Look how amazing—'

'Just listen!' Pippa repeated in exasperation. 'She's not all she seems, I'm telling you. For a start, look at all that metal in her face. No normal person goes around stuck with pins like that. Maybe she's got some wacky trick with magnets that makes all the dogs do what she wants, and she controls them with her stupid earrings. And then there's that horrible necklace thing. Anyone would think she was trying to look like a dog herself! And this is the oddest bit – when Mrs Prim told us about the Dalmatian, Minx went all . . . weird,' she finished lamely.

Dash was looking very doubtful. It was clear to him that poor Pippa was clutching at straws. She was so desperate to get rid of Minx and be Mrs Fudge's Number One Assistant again, that she was finding problems with the new girl where none existed.

Pippa was looking thoughtful. 'You were going to go out and look for the spotty dog yourself this morning, weren't you? Did you go?'

The dachshund shook his head, sending his silky ears flapping. 'No.' Pippa let out such a frustrated sigh that Dash added quickly, 'But now you come to mention it, I have been picking up some unusual scents recently.'

'You and your scents,' Pippa said, looking up at the ceiling. 'Sometimes it's better to use your *eyes*, you know. *I* am using my eyes, and I'm telling you Minx behaved very oddly indeed when Mrs Prim mentioned the spotty dog. Now, why would she do that?'

Dash was thoughtful. His tail tapped the floor gently and he licked his lips over and over as if he was tasting the information Pippa had just given him, although actually all he could think of was when he might get another of Minx's treats. He

tried to focus, to think of something to say to reassure his friend. 'Hmm,' he said eventually. 'Well, Minx did explain that she had learned all she knew from a dog whisperer. And she certainly seems to understand me—'

'WHAT?' Pippa cried. 'That's all I need! First she takes over my job, then she charms the customers, and now she's charmed you! I may as well go home right now.'

Dash rubbed his head against Pippa's long legs. 'Now, now,' he said. 'If you'll just let me finish. You're still my favourite. It's just that she seems to understand my body language or something. I can't really explain it . . .'

'Oh, great,' said Pippa, who was feeling far from consoled by this. 'So now you're telling me she's got magical powers?'

'Well, she did seem to understand what I was thinking yesterday. It was very odd, because she obviously couldn't actually hear a word I was saying. Not like you,' he added. He put his head on one side and gazed adoringly at Pippa. It was a large-eyed puppyish look designed to get the angry girl to see that he was on her side. It worked.

'Oh, Dash,' she cried, softening immediately. She gathered him into her arms for a cuddle. 'You'll stick by me, won't you? However marvellous this Minx turns out to be, you won't let her replace me, will you?'

Dash closed his eyes and rubbed his silky muzzle against Pippa's face. 'Absolutely not,' he assured her.

Although there is something special about this Minx, I can't deny it, he thought guiltily. She really does know dogs like no other human I've ever met.

10

A Dark and Foggy Night

Pippa sighed and dreamed of springtime as she weaved slowly in and out of the trees on Liquorice Drive on her skateboard that evening. The nights had been drawing in recently until there seemed to Pippa to be so much night there was hardly any day. And the days were so overcast and misty, it was as if they were jealous of the nights and were trying to imitate them.

It had been a long and difficult day: she had left Minx and Mrs Fudge tidying up the salon together, nattering away as though they had known each other all their lives. Mrs Fudge had barely noticed when Pippa had called out 'goodbye'. And Dash seemed glued to the new girl's side.

They don't need me any more, Pippa thought
miserably, as she got to the end of the lane. It's as
simple as that.

A heavy fog had settled in Crumbly-under-
Edge during the afternoon; it was white and thick,
as though someone had pulled down a blind over
the world. It made the town look fuzzy around
the edges and meant it was very hard to see where
you were going. It didn't bother Pippa though.
She could have found her way home with her eyes
closed, she knew the place so well. (Although the
other people in the town might have had something
to say about a ten-and-a-half-year-old girl
skateboarding after dark with her eyes shut. And I
wouldn't try it, if I were you.)

'I'm going to have to take charge of this Minx
situation,' Pippa muttered to herself. 'And if Dash
won't help me do any clue-finding, I shall have to
do it myself. There *must* be a link between Minx and
the spotty dog.' She thought over everything she
knew about the new girl so far. 'She turns up out

of the blue with some vague story about travelling and house-sitting. She knows all about dogs from a dog-whisperer person but she doesn't have a dog herself. She carries that *stupid* bag around with her everywhere, even when she goes to the loo – What was that?' She broke off in mid-sentence and stopped her skateboard.

She had just seen a very large ghostly shape. It had flitted past the lamp posts right ahead of her, but it hadn't made a sound. Pippa held her breath and listened. But all she could hear was her heart thumping so hard she was sure it was audible to the outside world as well. She put a blue woolly-gloved hand up to her chest and pressed down as if to stop the pounding.

There it was again! And this time she made out the shape: long, large, with a big head and long legs. It stopped, sat down and scratched itself and seemed to stare in her direction for a moment. Then quick as a flash, it was gone again.

Pippa let out the breath she had been holding and

it hovered in front of her face in a cloud. She picked up her skateboard and tiptoed silently into the road, checking all around her to see if the shape came back.

'It was that dog again,' she whispered. 'Gosh it's big! Bigger than any dog I've ever met. Faster too.'

Now, Pippa Peppercorn was *not* what you would call a scaredy-cat. (She was certainly not normally frightened of the dark: indeed, she had been known before now to creep out of her house after dark to do some very important spying.) But the combination of this dark winter evening, the fog and the ghostly shape of a large, strange dog seemingly roaming the streets alone would be enough to give anyone the collywobbles if you ask me, and it certainly did that to our Pippa. She thought about turning back to Mrs Fudge's, but then she remembered that Minx would still be there.

They'll just laugh at me, she thought glumly. She wondered about knocking on someone's door and telling them. But they'll just say I shouldn't be out on my skateboard in the dark anyway, she reasoned.

'Pippa?' A voice from behind her made her shoot into the air like a startled quail. (It's what quails do, you know. Terribly nervy little birds they are, you can take my word for it.)

'Oh!' she gasped, whirling round.

'Sorry, sweetness!' said the voice. 'It only me – Raphael. I was goin' to drop in on Mrs F. to see how she gettin' on. You OK, darlin'?' he asked, stepping forward and peering at Pippa. 'You shouldn't be out alone in this nasty weather. Let me take you home.'

'Thank you, Raphael,' Pippa said, trembling. 'That would be nice.'

She took the postie's hand and held on tight as he pushed off with his rollerblades and pulled her all the way home through the lanes.

When they arrived at Pippa's front door she said breathlessly, 'Raphael, I just saw that spotty dog

you've been talking about. And Mrs Prim's seen it too.'

Raphael looked alarmed. 'Oh mercy! Did it chase you? I has been keepin' a bit of a low profile since it ran after me, you know. And I is happy to tell you dat I has not seen it all of today. In fact, today has been de firs' day I has been able to deliver me letters without anyting happening to me.'

'Is that right?' Pippa felt bolder now that she was safely outside her own house. 'Well, that is very interesting.'

'Interesting! It's an almighty RELIEF is what it is, darlin'! But . . . but if you say you just saw it yoursel'?' His knees began knocking together. 'Oh no, Pippa. I is not likin' the idea o' dat monster out and about on a dark night like tonight.' He looked anxiously over his shoulder.

'Raphael, I have a theory about that dog,' Pippa said cautiously. 'I think it belongs to Mrs Fudge's new assistant, but for some reason she is pretending to have nothing to do with it. Maybe it's because it's

123

a really dangerous animal. Maybe –' She lowered
her voice. 'Oh my goodness, Raphael, what if it's a
trained *Killer Dog*?'

'Pippa! Don't you go about sayin' tings like dat!
You will frighten de Crumblies half out o' der wits,
girl!' Raphael shuddered. 'No, even I tink that your
over-active imag-in-a-tion is a-runnin' away wid
you now, sweetness. Let's change de subject. Tell
me what dis new girl is like.'

'Huh. Hardly a change of subject,' grumbled

Pippa. 'Why don't you come to Chop 'n' Chat
tomorrow and see for yourself.'

'You can count on me, sweetness,' said Raphael.
'It's my day off tomorrow, so I can stop by for a
proper chat. And if I see anyting un-us-ual in the
meantime, I'll keep you posted – cos that's what I
do!'

'Thank you, Raphael,' said Pippa, reaching up to
give him a hug. 'You'd better go home before you
catch cold.'

Pippa let herself into her house, giving the postie
a wave as he rollerbladed away. Raphael is always
on my side, she reassured herself. Everything's
going to be all right.

11

The Postie Whisperer

When Raphael arrived the next day, Minx was

silky soft ears

busy darting between a graceful, satiny saluki (whose silky soft ears needed gentle care and attention) and a cheeky miniature schnauzer (whose majestic moustache needed trimming).

majestic moustache

Mrs Fudge meanwhile was dealing with some tricksy human customers. Penelope Smythe wanted hair extensions (much against Mrs Fudge's better judgement). And a young boy was asking for his hair to be dyed green (such a devil of a colour to wash out if you decide you don't like it – which his teachers and parents most definitely wouldn't).

Muffles was sulking on the countertop, safely out of range.

As for Pippa, the poor girl was on tea duty again. She had also been set the task of sorting out the laundry and folding every single towel that Mrs Fudge possessed. Which was a lot of towels. She was just thinking of how she could persuade Dash to stop hero-worshipping Minx and actually give her a helping paw instead, when Raphael rollerbladed through to the salon.

'Hello, darlin's!' he called above the racket of the chatter and barking and clatter of teacups. 'More funny tings happenin' on my way through town this mornin', my lovelies. Listen to this: Mr Percy called me into his garden. His compost heap was a *ruin*!' Dash pricked up his ears at the mention of compost and twitched his nose in the air. 'Someting got in there in de night – he tinks it musta been badgers. All I sayin' is, dey musta been *giant* badgers . . .'

Raphael was saying. 'And then on my way here I crossed de park. Oh my, there was a terrible mess! All de bins had been knocked flyin'! I couldn't just go by and leave all de litter a-lyin' around like that. Someting not right, y'know – Oh!'

He stopped in his tracks when he saw Minx, who, Pippa noticed, had a funny expression on her face. What was it? Shock? Surprise?

'You must be de new assistant?' Raphael said. 'I been hearin' about you! The whole town's tongues are a-waggin', girl!'

'All good, I hope?' Minx said, with a shaky smile. Then she winked.

And the minute she winked, something very strange happened to Raphael. His eyes widened, his cheeks darkened. He opened and closed his mouth, but no sound came out. Then his knees seemed to sag and give way under him, and he sank backwards into a twirly-whirly chair (which thankfully was there to break his fall). Finally he let out a loud contented sigh and said softly, 'Oh, yes. All good. All very good.'

Pippa watched, first with astonishment, then with disbelief and finally with annoyance.

'Don't tell me, she's a postie whisperer too,' she muttered.

'What was that you were saying about the park, Raphael?' Mrs Fudge asked.

But the postman's attention was firmly fixed on

Minx. 'So, where are you from?' he asked her, a twinkle in his eye.

Minx faltered. 'I – oh. You know, here and there . . .'

'Well, I sure can't be de only one when I say I is glad you has come *here* for now!' chortled Raphael.

Minx lowered her eyelashes and bit her lip.

'Yeah, I think I might be hanging about for a bit.'

Raphael beamed. 'If you need anyting, let me know. I could show you round, maybe? I knows all de gossip and all de news.'

'I'm sure you do,' said Minx, smiling coyly. 'You being the postie and all that.'

'Yeah, man! I'll keep you posted, darlin''—'

'Oh for goodness sake!' spluttered Pippa. But she was interrupted by the owner of the saluki.

'She's heaven-sent, this girl is! Absolute gold dust! No one has ever groomed my Sukie so beautifully before.'

'Woof, woof!' agreed the saluki.

'I must say I could do with another cup of tea,' Penelope Smythe chattered.

'So are you going to dye my hair, or what?' butted in the young boy.

'Pippa dear, could you make a fresh pot? And fetch some more towels, there's a love,' Mrs Fudge called over the racket.

'Miaaaaoooooow!' protested Muffles, before

sliding off the counter and slinking away from the chaos.

Pippa exchanged a glance with Dash. As usual he knew what his friend was thinking, so he followed her.

'What do you make of that?' she asked him when they were safely in the kitchen.

Dash put his head on one side. 'What do you mean?'

'What I mean is, what do you think about how Raphael reacted to Minx just then?' Pippa said impatiently.

Dash did the doggy equivalent of shrugging his shoulders, which was to lower his head slightly and look up at Pippa from under his eyebrows.

Pippa huffed and said, 'Didn't you notice? She only had to *look* at him and he went all gooey and stupid! He was behaving like an IDIOT!'

Dash jumped down and nuzzled Pippa's legs. 'Now, now. Don't start that nonsense again,' he said gently.

 132

'It's not nonsense!' Pippa protested. Dash sat back on his haunches, his ears drooping. 'I just don't believe that Minx is as wonderfully flipping marvellous as everyone thinks she is,' Pippa went on. 'No one is that wonderful all of the time. Even Mrs Fudge has her off days. And did you notice how Minx didn't answer Raphael when he asked her where she comes from? And what about that idiotic Big Silver Bag? She carries it from room to room like she has the Crown Jewels in it or something. I tried taking it from her this morning to hang it up and she pretty much snatched it back off me. I think we should take a look inside it. She might have something really dangerous in there. A secret weapon, for example!'

Dash sat staring at Pippa helplessly, his head on one side. 'What can I say?' he sighed. 'I agree it is a *little* strange that she seems to have turned up out of nowhere . . . but that hardly makes her a criminal. And it definitely doesn't give us the right to go through her handbag.'

Pippa crossed her arms and narrowed her eyes. 'Well. I can see where your loyalties lie,' she said fiercely.

'Hey, is this a party? The best ones always end up in the kitchen!' Minx joked. She was leaning against the door frame with her arms crossed. She eyed Pippa questioningly and then winked at Dash. 'How's my favourite pooch?' she said. The little dachshund immediately rushed to her side and sat to attention, his tail wagging. Minx crouched down to his height and rubbed her nose against his. Then she straightened up, put her hand in her Big Silver Bag, which was slung over her shoulder as usual, and brought out a biscuit in the shape of a small bone.

'Can you sit up and beg, I wonder?' said Minx.

'Ha!' said Pippa. 'Good luck getting him to do *that*.'

But Dash had risen up on his hind legs and was holding his paws in a begging posture, his little red tongue hanging out of the corner of his mouth.

 134

'Well done, Dash!' said Minx. 'All the pooches love my homemade treats,' she added, flicking a triumphant glance at Pippa.

Just what else have you got inside that bag of yours? thought Pippa. It can't be only dog treats that you don't want the rest of us to see . . . I'll find out, with or without Dash's help, she told herself decisively, just you wait and see.

12

Minx Is Right Again

Pippa had decided, as part of her new surveillance plan, that she would be as friendly and charming to Minx as she possibly could be.

'That way I can lull her into a false sense of security,' she told Dash when she arrived after school the next day. 'Then she might confide in me or let something slip. You just watch me,' she added. 'I'm going to be as nice as pumpkin pie today.'

Dash merely nodded and wagged his tail slowly. He was secretly convinced that Pippa was making up silly theories now just because she didn't like Minx.

Pippa meanwhile was true to her word, and even

managed not to pass any comment on Minx's hair, which was scarlet red that day.

'We have a new client this afternoon, dears,' Mrs Fudge announced, when Pippa came into the salon. 'It's Mrs Peach's collie, Bella.'

'Mrs Peach is nice,' Pippa told Minx. 'She always gives good tips too.'

'Cool – but I thought you said she was a new client?' said Minx.

Mrs Fudge smiled. 'Mrs Peach herself has been having her hair done here for years, but this is Bella's first visit to the pooch-pampering parlour.'

Pippa nodded. 'I love Bella. She's a bit of a loony though – runs around town like a mad March hare! Talking of which,' she said, watching Minx carefully, 'I forgot to say. The weirdest thing happened to me on the way home the other night. It was really foggy, right, so I couldn't see that clearly, but I was sure I saw a *huge* dog racing around at the end of Liquorice Drive. It totally freaked me out! If Raphael hadn't—'

137

'What were you saying, Mrs Fudge?' Minx said loudly, cutting Pippa off. 'About Bella?' she prompted. 'If she's the sort of dog that can't sit still, she might not like being pampered.'

'Er, excuse me!' Pippa protested, 'I was talking about the strange dog just then and you—'

'That's very interesting, Minx dear,' said Mrs Fudge, giving Pippa one of her warning looks. 'Why do you say that?'

'Dogs can be nervy in new surroundings,' Minx explained. 'It depends on the breed, of course. Still, best to be prepared.'

Dash nodded, put his head on one side and said, 'She's right, you know, Pippa. Not all dogs are as easy to please as yours truly.'

Pippa rolled her eyes. 'Yes, we all know you're marvellous, Dash,' she said affectionately.

Minx laughed. 'He knows how to turn on the charm, doesn't he?'

Mrs Fudge smiled. 'Absolutely,' she agreed, bending down to ruffle Dash's fur. 'Let's hope Mrs

138

Peach's dog is even half as lovely.'

The doorbell sounded and Mrs Fudge called for 'All hands on deck!'

'I'll do Mrs Peach's hair,' she said. 'It's just her usual wash and blow-dry. Can you two manage Bella between you?'

Pippa and Minx nodded.

'Yes.'

'Yup.'

Dash nuzzled Pippa's leg. 'If you need any translation help, let me know.'

Minx was chewing a fingernail. 'There's something bothering me about this collie,' she said.

'But you haven't even met her yet!' Pippa protested, opening the door.

'It's what you said about the dog running around like a—'

Minx didn't get a chance to finish her sentence, as the minute Pippa opened the door a blurry black-and-white figure leaped at both girls, knocking Minx flying. Then it streaked down the hall, barking wildly.

'Oh!' Minx exclaimed, picking herself up.

Pippa noted this reaction with some satisfaction. Not marvellous with *every* kind of dog then, she thought.

A very out-of-puff Mrs Peach stood on the threshold to Mrs Fudge's house, her face etched with anxiety. 'I – I'm s-so terribly sorry,' she stammered between wheezy gasps for breath. Her hands fluttered at her throat. 'I think Bella's a – a little overexcited. She gets like this sometimes around new people and places.'

'No problem,' said Minx. 'I'll catch her.'

Pippa took Mrs Peach's hat and coat while Minx shot off towards the salon to catch the naughty

dog. Mrs Fudge and Dash followed.

'Mrs Peach,' said Pippa thoughtfully, 'has Bella been out at night recently?'

Mrs Peach frowned. 'No, of course not. What a funny question.'

'And she hasn't been running around the park without you? Knocking over bins or getting into mischief?'

'Absolutely not!' cried Mrs Peach indignantly. 'As if I would allow my dog to do such things.'

'Mrs Peach, dear!' Mrs Fudge appeared in doorway of the salon, looking flustered. 'Can you come? Bella is, er, being rather exuberant!'

Pippa and Mrs Peach scurried along to see Bella running round in ever decreasing circles, forcing a very angry Muffles, Minx, Dash and now Mrs Fudge into a huddle in the middle of the room.

Dash was barking, 'Get this lunatic out of here!'

Muffles's hackles were raised so high she looked more like a chimney sweep's brush than a cat, and

Mrs Fudge was waving her hands at Bella, crying, 'Sit! Heel! Calm down!'

Minx on the other hand was standing stock-still, staring at Bella with a fearsome look on her face. In fact, it almost looked as if she was snarling, Pippa thought. Much good *that* will do, she said to herself, and climbing up on to a chair she clapped her hands and yelled, 'SHUT UP!'

Unfortunately, the second she did this the noise went up a notch and Minx fixed *her* with the fearsome look, shaking her head and mouthing 'No' very clearly.

Mrs Peach grasped Pippa's arm. 'Bella doesn't like loud noises, dear.'

Pippa was beside herself. Here was the owner of a dog who was making a very loud noise telling her to be quiet and not make loud noises! It did not make one bit of sense to her. And if that wasn't bad enough, Minx was telling her off too.

Who does she think she is? Pippa thought, all her earlier promises to herself forgotten in the heat

 142

of the moment. Thinks she can tell me what to do, does she? Well, I'll show her . . .

She noticed that, in the commotion, Minx had left her Big Silver Bag lying in a corner by one of the twirly-whirly chairs.

Aha! thought Pippa. Here's my chance . . .

But she didn't have time to get to the bag because just then, the chaos and noise stopped, as though someone had flicked a switch to turn off the music during a game of musical statues.

Minx had managed to grab hold of Bella's collar and had made her sit. She was now looking deeply into the dog's eyes, the snarl still playing around the edges of her mouth. The collie was tilting her head, looking sidelong at Minx, as if it were a naughty child who had been ticked off by a teacher, and was accepting the reprimand with good grace. Pippa teetered precariously on one foot as she had been caught taking the first step towards the Big Silver Bag. She held her breath while she fought to regain her balance before anyone could ask what she was doing.

But she needn't have worried, for everyone was gazing at Minx in awe and total silence. The instant that Minx seemed satisfied that Bella had got the message about how to behave properly, she gently let go of the dog's collar. Then Dash and Mrs Fudge quietly backed away and Muffles took full advantage of her new-found freedom to bolt soundlessly from the room. (She knew better than to try to have the last hiss in a situation as volatile as this.)

'Good girl,' said Minx, breaking the silence. She was still holding Bella's gaze. 'Pippa,' she said, 'come and clip a lead on to Bella for me.'

Pippa was so relieved not to be caught sneaking a peek in the bag that she obeyed Minx without comment, taking a spare lead from a drawer where Mrs Fudge kept all manner of doggy accessories for her poochy clients. She clipped it on to Bella's collar, keeping the collie on a short rein. Minx gestured to Pippa to follow her out of the room with Bella, and Dash trotted behind at a safe distance.

As they walked out, Pippa shot a shifty glance in the direction of the bag. She was sure she had noticed something poking out of the top. She checked that Minx was not looking back to see what she was doing and then craned her neck.

There's more than dog biscuits in there, she thought. I wonder why she doesn't want us to see.

Dash nudged the back of her legs as they went outside and said in a low growl, 'I told you, that girl knows what she is doing. Mind you, what a

145

ridiculous hound. I tried to tell Bella to shut up, but do you know what she said?'

Minx turned around and butted in. 'Bella's just behaving naturally for a collie, you know.'

Pippa swallowed drily. She was not as convinced as Dash was that Minx couldn't understand every word he said.

Minx went on. 'Collies are working dogs. Sheepdogs mostly.' She paused and then gave a little snigger. 'I know it sounds mad, but cos they're bred to herd sheep, well . . . sometimes they just can't help – herding!'

Pippa's eyes boggled. 'So you mean – Bella was herding Dash and Mrs Fudge and Muffles back there?'

Minx nodded slowly.

Pippa burst out laughing.

Minx shrugged. 'It's not funny. Poor Bella's confused. I'll need to ask Mrs Peach if it's happened before. But hey, in the meantime, we need to remember that she might get like this if there are

lots of other people and animals around, OK? So can we deal with her quietly and without too many distractions? Let's shampoo her in the garden today and towel her down. The dryer might freak her out.'

Dash looked at Pippa sympathetically.

'Don't,' Pippa warned him.

'What?' he said, innocently.

'You were going to say "I'm afraid Minx is right" again, weren't you?' Pippa grumbled.

But Dash merely flicked his ears and soundlessly trotted off down the garden with Minx and Bella.

13

More Poochy Problems

It was to be a few days before Pippa would have another chance to get her hands on the Big Silver Bag. This was mainly because Chop 'n' Chat was as hectic as ever, which meant that Pippa was kept very busy and she simply did not have the time to snoop around.

She had, however, not forgotten about her bewildering experience on that foggy night when Raphael had come to her rescue. And the memory of this, combined with her worries about what Minx was keeping hidden in her bag, went round and round in her mind until she began to convince herself that the two things were linked.

One day Pippa arrived to find that the salon was

very quiet. Minx had not yet arrived, and the only customer was Coral Jones, who was sitting in the kitchen, snivelling into a hanky while she confided in Mrs Fudge, who had her arm around her. She was listening patiently while Coral wailed and blew her nose and repeated, 'I don't know what to do.'

'What is it?' Pippa asked, concerned. 'And where is Winston?' she added, looking around for Coral's pug.

Coral looked up at Pippa. Her face was streaked with smudged make-up and her eyes were shining with tears. At the mention of the pug's name, more tears sprang out of the poor lady's eyes and her mouth twisted into a clown's mask of misery, and she began blubbing noisily.

'Winston is the reason Coral's so upset, dear,' said Mrs Fudge gently, rubbing Coral's back and giving Pippa one of her looks.

Pippa gave Mrs Fudge one of her own looks back and shrugged, mouthing, 'Sorry – I didn't know!'

'Why don't you put the kettle on, Pippa, please?' Mrs Fudge asked. 'I think we could do with a fresh pot.'

Pippa huffed and stomped her way over to the stove. 'All I ever do is make the tea,' she muttered. 'Why can't she ask Minx to do that for a change?' She paused and thought for a moment. 'Actually, that's a point: where *is* Minx? Typical! On the one day I could have some time to do a bit of detective work, she's not here!' She clattered the kettle moodily into the sink and wrenched hard to turn on the tap.

Coral jumped at the noise and whimpered, 'I'm sorry, Pippa. It's awful of me to sit here and cry like this. But I'm at the end of my tether. Darling Winston just won't go out for walks any more. The minute I open the front door he goes crazy, barking and whining and shivering and shaking. I don't know what's wrong with him. I've been walking him round and round my tiny back garden for the past week. But then last night, when I wanted him to go out for his last walk of the day, he spotted something in the bushes and wouldn't even go out into his own garden!'

She blew her nose loudly into her hanky.

'Well, dear,' said Mrs Fudge eventually, 'I can see that is rather inconvenient, but it's no reason to—'

'But it's not only Winston who is frightened to go out!' Coral interrupted, her voice escalating in pitch. 'I – I saw something out there too last night and . . . and I *heard* it as well,' she added in a whisper.

Muffles opened one eye and shot Coral an inquisitive look, then closed her eye again and settled back to sleep.

'What?' Pippa asked. 'What did you see and hear?'

Coral sniffed loudly and said, 'A huge beast! It howls like a wolf! And it runs faster than any animal I've ever seen. And it's covered in—'

'Black spots?' finished Pippa.

Dash came trotting in at that moment. He had been out in the garden chasing squirrels ('I like to keep in shape,' had been his explanation when questioned on this pastime. 'What shape is that exactly?' Pippa had retorted. 'Sausage-shape?')

'Oh dear!' he remarked, on seeing Coral's tear-smudged face. 'What on earth is going on? Not another dog-napping, I hope?' he added grimly.

'No,' said Pippa, bending low to whisper back to him. 'Winston has been scared by the big spotty dog!'

Coral blew her nose again, causing Dash to start in surprise. 'What am I going to do, Mrs Fudge? Do you think anyone else has seen the beast? I was thinking about asking Raphael. He normally knows everything that's going on.'

Mrs Fudge was drumming her fingers

thoughtfully on the tabletop. 'Raphael may well have seen the same animal himself,' she said. 'He was being chased by a spotty dog recently, but he says he hasn't seen it for a while. In any case, Raphael is not an expert on dog behaviour . . .'

'But you know someone who is,' chipped in Dash.

Pippa rolled her eyes, while Mrs Fudge brightened at Dash's words. 'Yes, Dash – I mean, Coral, I've just had a thought,' she said, quickly. 'Have you met my new assistant, Minx, yet?'

'No,' said Coral, sniffing. 'But I hear she's an absolute marvel. I wanted to see if she had any advice on how to calm poor Winnie down.'

Pippa grimaced.

'She *is* a marvel!' Mrs Fudge agreed. And then, catching the sour look on Pippa's face, 'I mean, she's been quite a help. Of course, I don't know what I would do without Pippa . . .'

Dash nudged Mrs Fudge to point out she was straying from the subject of Coral's troubled dog.

153

'Anyway,' said Mrs Fudge, getting out her gold pocket watch to check the time. 'Where on earth *is* Minx this morning? Has she called?'

Pippa shook her head and concentrated on making her face as blank as possible – which was hard, as she had been beginning to feel distinctly pleased that Minx had not turned up or called to explain her absence.

'Oh dear,' said Mrs Fudge. 'I do hope she's not unwell. Pippa, will you give her a ring?'

Pippa dragged her feet sulkily into the salon and flicked through the phone book until she had found Minx's telephone number. 9-8-6-4. As she dialled, she found herself hoping that Minx might have changed her mind about coming to work in the salon ever again . . .

14

It's in the Bag!

'Hey, everyone! Sorry I'm late!'

The voice made Pippa jump and drop the telephone receiver with a heavy *clunk* on the counter. It also brought Dash, Mrs Fudge and Coral running from the kitchen.

Minx was in the hallway, hanging up her coat, her Big Silver Bag slung over her shoulder as usual. Her hair was the orange of a beech leaf in autumn, and she was wearing tights to match. One of the legs had a huge hole in it, Pippa noticed. The rest of Minx's clothes were black as normal, but they looked decidedly more crumpled than they usually did and she wasn't wearing her polka-dot scarf.

Minx's cheerful manner immediately annoyed

Pippa. 'What time do you call this?' she demanded, her brow knitted into a dark frown. She crossed her arms and tapped her foot impatiently.

But Dash had already scurried up to Minx, his tail swishing back and forth in greeting, his nose sniffing at the assistant's feet.

'Interesting,' he was saying. 'Smells like—'

'Hi, Dash! I brought you something . . .' Minx reached into her bag and fished out a treat for him which he gobbled down and seemed instantly to forget what he had been about to comment on.

And Mrs Fudge was crying, 'Minx, my dear! I was beginning to worry. Are you quite all right?'

But Minx was now busy being fussed over by Coral, who was behaving like an excited puppy. 'Oh! You must be Minx. I'm so pleased to meet you! I need your help, you see . . .'

Come on then, Minx, thought Pippa. Let's see you solve this one.

As Coral went into detail about the spotty dog, Minx's face seemed to develop a greenish tinge

which clashed rather hideously with her orange hair.

'We were hoping you might be able to come round to our place and see if you could catch the mystery dog. It should be returned to its rightful owners,' said Coral.

'Wow – er – I don't know, that dog sounds, like, super-spooky,' Minx stammered. She scratched her right ear nervously. Her eyes shifted from left to right as though she was worried the scary dog might actually be in Mrs Fudge's kitchen. 'But, hey! I've got an idea!' she announced, brightening. 'Bring your Winston here and I can take a look at him and maybe help him get over his nerves? I know a few tricks to calm a dog down.'

'She can't!' Pippa protested. 'Didn't you hear what Coral said? Winnie won't even leave the house. How is she going to bring him *here*?'

Mrs Fudge laid a hand on Pippa's arm and looked at her over the top of her spectacles. 'Maybe we should hear what Minx has to say, dear.'

157

'Bring him here in a box,' continued Minx calmly. 'Dogs feel calmer in small, dark spaces. Once he's curled up tight like that, he won't worry so much.'

'She's right,' said Dash, earning another glare from Pippa.

Coral brought her pug into Chop 'n' Chat later that day. She had tempted him into a cardboard box with some of his favourite doggy chocolate drops, and had made the box comfy with a soft folded blanket. When Pippa opened the door, she could hear contented snuffles and snores coming from the box, and Coral was beaming with joy.

'It worked a treat!' she trilled, as she struggled over the threshold with the box in her arms. 'He fell asleep as soon as I put him in the car.'

'Here, let me help you,' Pippa said, holding out her arms.

Between them they set the box carefully on the ground, then Pippa opened the box and peeped

inside. Dash jumped up and put his paws on the side of the box and peered in as well.

'Aw! Doesn't Winnie look cute!' cooed Pippa.

He certainly did. He was curled in a ball, his little tail rolled up in a spiral like a snail's shell and his paws tucked neatly underneath him. His eyes were closed and he was making soft snorty noises as he snoozed.

'Mmm,' said Dash. 'I suppose you could call it that.'

Pippa grinned. 'Now who's jealous?'

Minx came out to say hello. 'Hey! It worked!' she exclaimed. 'And how is the little guy now that he's here?'

Pippa glowered and put her finger to her lips, 'Shh!' she said. 'He's sleeping.'

'Rrruff?' Winston opened one eye and saw Dash and Pippa standing over him. He stood up groggily and stretched each leg in turn, then his tail quivered with happiness and he stood up on his hind legs to greet Dash with a friendly sniff.

Something seemed to catch his attention as he did this though. He began sniffing the air around and above Dash instead. Whatever the smell was, it had an immediate effect on the small pug: he began to whimper, his ears went back and his tail went limp. Then he narrowed his eyes and the whimper grew to a growl and then crescendoed into a cacophony of barking that made Pippa cover her ears with her hands and had Dash scurrying for cover behind her legs.

Coral swiftly scooped her dog into her arms and began stroking him and crooning to him. Eventually he seemed to realize he was safe and he calmed down.

'What was *that* all that about?' Pippa muttered to Dash.

160

'Tell you later,' the dachshund replied, nodding in Minx's direction.

The new assistant was taking charge of the situation. Gently, she reached out her hand to touch him, but Winston began whimpering again. Minx swiftly withdrew her hand. 'Right,' she said hastily. 'Let's get him into the salon and I'll have a proper look at him.'

But Winston was not keen on staying put. He struggled and wriggled so much that Coral could not keep a hold of him, and with a final squirm he had dropped down on to the floor and was running out to the back door, barking and snarling and baring his teeth.

Pippa hung back with Dash as the others ran after the pug at full pelt.

'What *is* Winston saying?' she insisted, fixing Dash with a determined expression. 'You have to tell me.'

'I – I don't think he likes Minx very much,' Dash said. He looked down sheepishly, as if reluctant to admit what Winston had said. 'He says she smells like the scary dog,' he said eventually.

'I knew it!' Pippa cried, punching the air. 'She must be his owner.'

'And – look,' Dash said haltingly. He was staring at something lying in the middle of the floor. Something large, shiny and silvery.

'Minx's bag!' Pippa whispered. She could not believe her luck. As she picked it up, she had to concentrate very hard on containing her excitement.

'Quick!' she said to Dash in a low voice, and nodded towards the living room.

Pippa closed the door very, very carefully behind them, making sure that the catch did not click as she turned the handle. Then she put her ear to the door to make sure no one had followed her. She could only hear the others calling desperately to Winston, who appeared to have hidden himself somewhere in the kitchen.

'Dash,' she hissed, 'keep your super-sharp ears out for anyone heading this way, OK?'

Dash nodded, and took up his station by the door, his head pressed against it.

Pippa knelt down and put the Big Silver Bag on the floor, her heart thudding. I must be quick, she thought. She unzipped the bag, wincing at the noise it made; it seemed to her nervous ears to be a sound amplified to unnaturally loud levels. The top of the bag fell open and Pippa peered in.

She did not know what it was that she had been expecting to find – maybe a book about how to hypnotize dogs. Minx obviously had some way of cheating when it came to making all the dogs in Crumbly-under-Edge fall under her spell (well, apart from Winston). But Pippa couldn't have been more surprised at what was inside. She pulled out each item in turn.

'Enough dog biscuits to feed a dog for months – she can't need to lug all this lot around just to please you, Dash,' she said with raised eyebrows.

'She doesn't just give them to me, she—' began Dash.

But Pippa was pulling more things out of the bag. 'Hey, look at this! A pair of old boots – they look as though something's chewed them . . . and a couple of dirty towels . . . a workman's overalls? Hang on a minute,' Pippa paused as alarm bells began ringing loudly in her mind. 'Old boots, overalls, dirty towels – oily ones too – wasn't that what the mechanic said had gone missing? And look at this! Loads of spare clothes, all like the ones Minx is already wearing. Urgh!' She held up a handful of pairs of tights, some black, some black with white spots on, some white with black spots and one orange pair. Quite a few of them seemed to be covered in sludgy, gloopy slime. 'What on earth *is* this stuff?'

Dash sniffed at the muck on the clothes. 'I – I think it's compost,' he said slowly.

'Raphael said an animal had been through someone's compost, didn't he? Oh! Hang on a minute, what's this?' Pippa rootled in the bottom of the bag, trying to get her fingers around something. She brought out the object and put it on the floor. 'A dog tag?' she said, very puzzled now. Then she sneered. 'Ha! Minx should put it on that stupid necklace she wears. I always thought it looked like a dog's collar.'

'What does it say on it?' Dash asked.

'It says "Polka". Hey, that's Minx's surname,' Pippa said, looking at Dash quizzically. She turned it over. 'And there's a phone number. It looks familiar.' She closed her eyes tight and thought about the number she had dialled earlier.

9-8-6-4.

'Got you,' breathed Pippa. She opened her eyes and held the tag up to Dash. 'This is the proof we need,' she said.

'Proof of what?' asked Dash, puzzled.

'Minx is the owner of the spotty dog,' she said. 'And she's embarrassed because she's lost control of it. She's been hiding the evidence in this stupid bag as she goes. First the mechanic's things, then the smelly compost, and now she's removed the dog's tag so that no one can link it to her. It's running riot and scaring all the Crumblies and their dogs and she doesn't know what to do. She's hiding here at Chop 'n' Chat, pretending to be a marvellous dog whisperer and getting everyone on her side so that they won't put two and two together and realize the horrible hound is hers! I bet she's training it with her "special powers" to do something truly evil, like, like . . . catch all the small fluffy creatures in Crumbly-under-Edge and take them away to be made into, into . . . fur hats or something!' Pippa finished, with a sinister wiggle of her eyebrows.

Dash drew his head away from the door and looked at her questioningly. 'I do think you're going a little over the top, Pippa. Is it a crime to own a boisterous dog?' he asked. 'Plenty of people come here with their own doggy problems.'

But Pippa wasn't listening; her turquoise eyes were shining in triumph. 'Come on, Dash,' she said, shoving everything back into the bag and jumping up. 'That Minx Polka has got some explaining to do.'

15

The Missing Post Bag

Pippa and Dash walked into the salon to find Coral cradling Winston in her arms.

'Poor Winston,' Minx was saying. 'He's had an awful shock. I suggest we gradually reintroduce him to the outside, giving him a treat for every step he takes out of the door. He will soon associate going out with getting a treat, and then you'll have a happy hound again who will do as he is told!'

'Yeah, and what would you know about happy hounds?' Pippa interrupted with a sneer, getting ready to show everyone her discovery. But Mrs Fudge stepped in between her and Minx and looked very stern.

'Pippa!' she exclaimed. 'Minx is in the middle of a diagnosis. Let her finish, please.'

Pippa opened her mouth to protest, 'A dia-what-nis?' But Mrs Fudge glared at her.

Minx scratched her right ear and went on, 'Er, yes. As I was saying, Winston just needs a bit of special attention, Coral – and lots of praise! He'll soon be right as rain,' she finished, shooting Pippa a nervous glance.

'That sounds wonderful,' Coral said, in a voice hushed with awe. 'Thank you.'

Pippa's hair was fizzing and crackling with indignation: she had an important announcement to make about this fraud of an assistant!

'B-b-but she's a hypocrite—' she tried again, only to have Mrs Fudge shake a finger at her to be quiet while Minx carried on and on.

No one was listening to her!

'And if Winston finds it all too much too soon, maybe for now you could take him out in one of those shopping trolleys on wheels, or a little bag, just until he's ready to be let off the lead for a good run around?'

Even Dash choked at that. 'A dog in a BAG? Whatever next . . .'

'Yeah, like a BIG SILVER BAG,' Pippa said loudly. She held up the bag as evidence for all to see.

Dash let out a sharp bark in agreement. 'You're right, Pippa. This girl needs taking down a peg or two.'

'Eh?' said Minx, finally looking up at them properly. Then, seeing what Pippa was holding, she went bright red and shouted, 'What are you doing with my things?' She pushed past Mrs Fudge and stormed across to Pippa, snatching her bag.

Mrs Fudge put a hand on Minx's arm and said sternly, 'Pippa! I am disappointed in you!'

'But, Mrs Fudge!' she protested. 'I think you should see this.'

'I can't believe you! Going through my stuff without asking! I'm not staying any longer, Mrs

Fudge,' said Minx, tears spilling over her long dark lashes. 'I can't work here if I'm not trusted.'

And with that, she ran from the salon, leaving Mrs Fudge staring after her, her face as pale as her snow-white fluffy hair.

Coral looked extremely uncomfortable. She cleared her throat and said, 'I — I think we should go and, ah, leave you to it.' She made sure Winston was comfy in the cardboard box, then she left with many embarrassed mutterings about how sorry she was and how she would see them soon.

Mrs Fudge sat down on one of her twirly-whirly chairs and stared vacantly after Coral.

'Well, thank goodness for that,' said Pippa briskly. 'Now will you listen to me, Mrs Fudge?'

Dash jumped up and rested his paws on her shins. 'Pippa,' he said in a warning tone. 'I don't think this is the best time—'

'What have you done, Pippa?' Mrs Fudge cut across the little dog in a voice that was full of hurt. 'How could you upset Minx like that? She saved me

171

in my hour of need and now . . .' She tailed off and shook her head sadly. 'What will I do without her? I'll be run off my feet again. I'm too old to work that hard, Pippa.'

'But, Mrs Fudge!' Pippa protested. 'You have to let me explain! Minx is a *fraud*!'

Mrs Fudge's face darkened and she was about to say something (thankfully she didn't as she might very well have come to regret it later) when there was a SLAM! And a shout of 'Oh my goodness to mercy!' And a rattling of rollerblades, and an 'Is anyone dere?'

Pippa thanked her lucky stars for the diversion and ran out into the hall to see Raphael, doubled over as he tried to get his breath back, puffing and panting and looking altogether very un-Raphael-like.

'Oh, Raphael! What's happened?' cried Pippa. Her stomach dropped suddenly as though she was in a very fast-moving rollercoaster. She had a distinctly nasty feeling that the day was about to turn from bad to worse.

Mrs Fudge was calling wearily from the salon, 'What is it?'

Raphael drew himself up to his full height and panted, 'It's terrible, Pippa sweetness. I is tellin' you, notin' dis bad has ever happen to me before!'

Dash scampered over to him and jumped up. 'Calm down, Raphael. Come in and catch your breath and then you can tell us everything. Whatever it is, I'm sure we'll be able to help.'

'I don't know if you can,' Raphael groaned, his head in his hands. 'You is not goin' to believe it, but someone has stolen me post bag!'

MISSING!

HAVE YOU SEEN THIS POST BAG?! (this one)

ANY INFORMATION CONTACT:
OHNO I HAVE LOST MY POST BAG@ RAPHAEL .ARGH!

Pippa gasped, her hands flying to her throat. 'No!' she said.

'Yes, oh yes, oh yes!' Raphael contradicted her, nodding vigorously. 'All me letters an' all me parcels. GONE!'

'Raphael, I think you'd better have a cup of tea,' said Mrs Fudge. 'I'm sure there's a logical explanation. Why would anyone round here want to steal the post?'

'I know, I know!' Raphael cried. 'But somebody has. And now I is goin' to have to tell ever-y-bo-dy, isn't I?'

'Raphael, you mustn't worry,' said Dash. 'Pippa and I are tippity-top at solving mysteries. We'll track down your post bag in no time.'

'What about Minx?' Raphael asked, blushing slightly. 'I should tell her too, shouldn't I, sweetness? She is so good at solvin' tings. I hear she has helped Mrs Peach and Mrs Prim and—'

'Yes,' Pippa butted in. She grasped Raphael's sleeve and pulled him into the kitchen. 'But

Minx is out at the moment.'

'And it doesn't look as though she'll be coming back,' muttered Mrs Fudge.

'WHAT?' cried Raphael.

'We don't need Minx to help us,' Pippa went on hastily. 'After all, this doesn't sound like a dog-related problem, does it? Start from the beginning. Tell us EVERYTHING.'

Mrs Fudge sighed heavily. 'Yes,' she said. 'Dash and Pippa will help you. I'll make that tea. I know I could do with some. And I think a slice of sponge cake would not go amiss.'

She tottered off to the cupboards to fetch down a cake tin while Raphael recounted his morning. Dash sat quietly at Pippa's feet and listened carefully with his head on one side.

'I went to de post office early, just like I normally do,' said the postie. 'I gets me letters and parcels what has been sent from de main office and I starts to pack me post bag. Then what happens?' He drifted off for a moment. 'Oh, that's it! The phone

175

in the office rings. I get distracted, I runs to answer . . . and when I comes back – ALL DE POST IS GONE!'

'That's it?' Dash asked, rather scornfully. 'No clues? No trace of anyone creeping in while you were on the phone? Come on. There must be something you can give us to go on.'

Raphael accepted a cup of hot tea from Mrs Fudge and took a noisy slurp. 'Aaah, that be makin' me feel better already, my darlin',' he added, smiling gratefully at the little old lady. 'It's a miracle what a nice cup o' tea can do.' He took another quick sip and nibbled at a slice of cake and then continued. 'Hmm, well, I am in a panic, so I race right here, don't I?' he said. 'But let me tink a minute.' He wiped his mouth on the back of his sleeve and looked up at the ceiling in deep thought.

Dash began to bang his tail impatiently against the floor, and Pippa drummed her fingers on the kitchen table. Raphael was usually so observant, she mused. He knew all the names of all the people in Crumbly-under-Edge and he was always such a good source of gossip. It was very odd that he had not noticed any clues before rushing away from the scene.

Eventually Dash coughed to break the silence and said, 'What about footprints? Anything dropped on the floor? Any unusual smells?'

Raphael looked very miserable. He shook his head, and his hair, which was normally so bouncy, flopped woefully over his eyes. 'I don't know about any smells or such like. But I don't see no clues, man.'

'Never mind, Raphael,' Pippa consoled him. 'Dash will help by tracking any scents he picks up, and I can do a spot of detective work around the town on my skateboard. Is it all right, Mrs Fudge, if we go now?'

Mrs Fudge nodded. 'Yes, you do that,' she said. 'I've got Kurt coming in a minute, but my other appointment has cancelled, thankfully, so I'll be able to manage.'

Pippa felt a twinge of guilt at leaving her old friend alone. But, she told herself, this is an important crime that needs solving. And if I can crack it, I can remind Mrs Fudge that I'm a very useful assistant too. Then maybe she'll forget all about Minx Polka and everything can get back to the way it was at Chop 'n' Chat before that freaky fraud turned up on the scene.

16

Intruder Alert!

Pippa took her skateboard, and Dash balanced neatly on the end, his ears flowing elegantly in the breeze as the two friends zipped along behind Raphael on his rollerblades.

'I'll take you to the sortin' office first, darlin's,' Raphael called out over his shoulder. 'You'll need a good sniff around there, won't you, Dash?'

The dachshund barked in agreement, 'Definitely!'

Although Pippa had promised the postie that Dash would assist them, she couldn't help remembering how Dash had not been brilliant at using his supposedly sensitive snout the last time there had been unusual goings-on in Crumbly-under-Edge. But I can't tell Raphael that, she thought. He needs all the encouragement he can get.

Once they arrived at the sorting office, things were worse for poor Raphael than any of them could have imagined. Not only was there no sign of his sack of letters and parcels for the day, but in his absence someone had clearly come back, and had ransacked his small fridge where he kept milk for his tea and food for his lunch and snacks. Empty wrappers littered the floor, a bottle of milk lay smashed, with a river of milk flowing and spreading into a small lake under Raphael's desk, and the fridge door was hanging off its hinges as though whoever it was had swung from it like a monkey on a branch.

Dash was off round the office in a flash, pointy nose to the ground, feathery ears twitching for any unusual sounds. 'I'm rather baffled, to be honest,' he murmured, as he snuffled from one corner of the room to the other. 'If I didn't know better I'd say you have had a dog in here, Raphael,' he said

finally, sitting back on his haunches with his shiny
little head on one side.

Pippa rolled her eyes. 'Da-ash!' she moaned. 'He
does have a dog in here – YOU!'

Dash cocked one ear and growled impatiently. 'I
know that!' he snapped. 'I mean *another* dog.'

'So, what does this "other" dog smell like?' asked
Pippa.

'Well, it's difficult to
say,' said Dash. 'The scent
is heavily masked by the
smell of sausage rolls,
milk, chocolate and
many other things
that have come from
Raphael's fridge.'

Pippa was tapping her foot angrily. 'If it's a dog, you must know which dog it is, you just don't want to admit it,' she said accusingly. 'So you're going to lead us on a wild goose chase, aren't you? Just like that time when we went around the whole of Crumbly-under-Edge looking for clues and ended up back where we had started!'

'Now, hold on a minute, young lady,' Dash growled, his hackles rising. 'There are a lot of doggy smells in here, actually. And it's difficult to separate them all out.'

Raphael had been looking anxiously from the dog to the little girl and decided he should step in before a full-scale argument broke out.

'I is sure Dash knows what he's talkin' about,' said Raphael hastily. 'The ting is, I have a lot of people comin' in an' out o' here and some of them's bringin' their dogs too. Say, for example, if somebody is on holiday when a parcel arrives for them? I might put a little card through the door to say "Come and get your parcel from the office

when you are home". And then they come and they might be bringin' their dog with them when they comes to collect it!'

'Right,' said Pippa crossly. 'So we need you to look for *more* clues, Dash.'

But Dash was frowning, his ears flat, his tail low to the ground. 'You don't get it, Pippa. There is one scent in particular which is ringing alarm bells somewhere in the back of my mind. They are very faint alarm bells just now, but if I concentrate, I am sure I will be able to work out what this scent is trying to tell me.'

Pippa threw up her hands in exasperation. 'Dash!' she exclaimed. 'Stop wasting time.'

Dash put on his most winning expression. 'You know what I think this is, Pippa?' he asked.

'No,' Pippa snapped.

Dash blinked appealingly and nuzzled his friend's knee. 'I think this is another one of those two-bone problems.'

'Eh?' exclaimed Raphael. 'What on eart' is a

"two-bone prob-lem" when it is at home?'

Pippa rolled her eyes. 'A two-bone problem is Dash's way of avoiding admitting he cannot solve this mystery,' she muttered.

Dash lowered his head to show how Pippa had hurt his feelings. 'That is simply not true,' he protested. 'A two-bone problem is a particularly tricky puzzle which requires my total concentration. And for total concentration, there is nothing more helpful than a couple of bones to crunch on – calms the mind and gets the grey matter whirring, you know,' he added with a raise of one eyebrow.

Raphael nodded wisely. 'I tink the little fella be right, Pippa darlin'. If it be bones dat work for him, den bones he shall have. For me it would be some good tunes and a nice hot cuppa, y'know?'

Pippa tutted impatiently. 'Very well. I'll get you your bones, but you had better crunch them pretty flipping fast, Dash. We need to find the bag before any of the Crumblies realize

 184

their post is missing! We can't have you getting into trouble, Raphael. You might lose your job! And I for one am not going to stand by and watch that happen.'

17

A Three-Bone Problem?

Back at Chop 'n' Chat, Pippa waited while Dash crunched his way noisily through his first bone.

'So?' she asked sarcastically, as he smacked his chops and looked around for the second one. 'Any sudden flashes of brilliance? Any super-intelligent brainwaves?'

'Er, I did say it was a *two*-bone problem, Pippa,' said Dash, eyeing the second bone greedily. 'So perhaps you should save your questions until I have actually had two bones?'

Before Pippa could think of a suitably cutting response to the cheeky little dachshund, a terrible commotion broke out in Liquorice Drive. Raphael was rollerblading at top speed towards them, hair

flying around his head like a mass of angry snakes. 'STOP! Stop!' he cried. 'No time for Dash's two-bone tinkin' time. Listen! I found me bag and all me letters but it's happened again, sweetness, and this time it's not just me who's had me stuff pinched! This is turnin' into a *three*-bone problem, if you ask me!'

'Don't give him any ideas,' muttered Pippa. But out loud she said, 'Where was your bag, Raphael?'

'It was in the hedge in Marble Wainwright's garden!' he cried. 'And de letters an' parcels and tings were all over de road – all trampled and trod into de mud! But that is not the worst of it, I tell you.'

Marble was hobbling up the drive behind Raphael, quite out of breath with the effort of keeping up with the postie. 'My house! My house!' she was yelling.

Mrs Fudge had heard the racket and was at the door at once, with a still-bedraggled Kurt standing in her shadow.

'I've been burgled!' Marble shouted.

'WHAT?' cried Mrs Fudge and Pippa in unison.

Marble's puddingy face was as white as a white marshmallow and the top of her potatoey nose had gone bright red. She was flapping her hands and her bottom lip was quivering in distress. 'My house, I tell you, has been *burgled*!' she repeated uselessly.

'Come in and sit down, both of you,' said Mrs Fudge.

The bewildered postie and the flustered Marble scurried into the kitchen. Marble wouldn't stop babbling on the way, gesticulating wildly as she told her story of how she had been out for a walk with Snooks and had come back to find her house in a terrible state.

'The back door was hanging off its hinges!' she wailed, flopping into a rocking chair.

'How on earth—?' gasped Mrs Fudge.

Raphael chipped in. 'Marble had me fix her a cat flap in de back door – for Snooksie to come and go whenever he fancy,' he explained to the puzzled

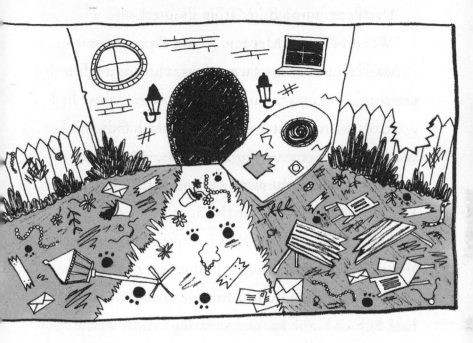

onlookers. (You mean so that lazy Marble didn't have to bother with letting him out, Pippa thought.) 'I am tinkin' de intruder is gettin' in through dere,' Raphael finished.

'But what kind of an intruder could fit in through a cat flap?' Pippa scoffed.

'That is just de point – the intruder did not fit through! That be why de door is *hangin' off its hinges* just like Marble tell you, man!'

Marble was nodding. 'It looks as though whoever it was misjudged the space, forced themselves through and ended up wrenching the door off in the process.'

'Hold on a minute!' interrupted Mrs Fudge, her hands in the air. 'This is utter nonsense. What person in their right minds would think they could possibly fit through a cat flap?'

As Mrs Fudge asked that last question, an idea flashed into Pippa's mind. She thought about the things she had found in Minx's bag and what she had deduced. She looked at Dash. I can't wait for him to make up his mind, she thought. But Dash was looking at her too. They both had their eyebrows raised, and if you could have seen the inner workings of their brains, you would have noticed that they were both coming to the same conclusion in their minds

Pippa nodded slowly, as if reading Dash's thoughts, and Dash put his head on one side as if reading hers. Then, as one, they said:

'Unless the intruder is not a *person*.'

'What did you say?' said Marble, peering at Pippa curiously. 'I didn't quite catch that because of that mutt's barking.'

Dash opened his mouth to bark some more, but even if he had been allowed to say what was on his mind, I couldn't possibly tell you what it was, as it was decidedly rude. Luckily Pippa leaped in, raising her voice, and said, 'I said, what if it wasn't a person – who broke in, I mean?'

Marble made a derisive snorting noise, but Raphael put a hand on her arm and said, 'Wait a minute – what are you tinkin', Pippa girl?'

All eyes were on Pippa. She took a deep breath and twirled one of her long plaits as she thought for a moment, then glancing quickly at Dash (who gave a very slight nod to encourage her) she said, 'What if it was a dog?' She paused. 'A very large, *badly behaved* dog.'

Marble suddenly laughed aloud. 'I've heard of a cat burglar, but really!' she scoffed.

191

'You mean,' broke in Raphael, in hushed tones, 'like a very large, badly behaved white dog . . . with black spots?'

Pippa nodded. 'The Dalmatian,' she said.

Raphael, Marble, Kurt and Mrs Fudge gasped in unison.

'We need to follow that scent,' said Pippa, taking charge.

Dash barked in agreement. 'Elementary, my dear!' he said.

18

The Dotty Dalmatian

'Marble, darlin', said Raphael. 'You is goin' to have to take us to your house so we can gather de evidence. Hold on tight to Pippa and she'll take you on her skateboard. I will carry Dash.'

Pippa was rather indignant at the thought of carrying the heavy weight of Marble Wainwright along on her skateboard, but Raphael did not give her time to protest. He gathered Dash into his arms and set off, calling to Pippa to 'hurry along now, girl!'

Poor Pippa! It was certainly very hard work, skateboarding with Marble clinging on to her for dear life. But the thought of solving the mystery and catching the culprit (and thereby, she hoped, getting back into Mrs Fudge's good books, not to mention getting to the bottom of what Minx was up to) was enough to spur Pippa on, and they reached Marble's house in no time at all. Raphael and Dash were already there, taking a good look (and sniff) around.

The place was in an appalling state. The intruder had rampaged through the bushes, knocked over the flowerpots, crashed into the garden furniture and pushed over the bird table. The neatly tended lawn had great trenches gouged out of it, and when Pippa and Marble reached the back door Pippa saw that it was indeed hanging off its hinges and was banging against the door frame in the squally wintery wind.

'Did you see what had been taken?' Pippa asked her potato-faced neighbour.

'I – I was too scared to go inside,' Marble admitted, her bottom lip wobbling. 'I had been out walking Snooksie, as I told you. I came home, saw that I had been burgled and ran straight next door to my neighbour to ask her to look after Snooksie for me. Then I saw Raphael, so I asked him to help. I must go and check on the dog, actually,' she said. 'I'll be back in a moment.' And she scuttled next door to her neighbour's, leaving Pippa with Dash and the postie.

'Phew,' said Pippa. 'Now she's gone, we can have a proper conversation.' She tucked her skateboard under her arm in a business-like manner and turned to Dash. 'Any more clues?' she asked.

Dash's nose was so close to the ground he looked like a little red furry vacuum cleaner. His feathery tail was whirring round and round with enthusiasm; it definitely seemed as though he was on to something.

Eventually he sat back on his haunches and said, 'I can certainly pick up the same scent that I found at Raphael's and I am sure it is not one of the dogs we know, so that would suggest that the Dalmatian could be at fault. But what I don't understand is why a dog would commit a burglary.

You have to admit it is rather strange.'

Raphael was nodding vigorously. 'It is to-tally bon-kers, man! What does a dog want with me post bag, I is askin' you?'

'It plainly did not want anything with it,' Dash pointed out. 'You say you found all the letters and parcels strewn around Marble's garden. In fact, look! There's another one,' and he scampered over to a flattened rose bush that had a letter spiked on to one of its thorns.

Pippa chewed her bottom lip. 'Let's take a look inside Marble's house,' she suggested.

Once inside, it was clear that the intruder had ransacked the place. Every room looked as though a tornado had been through it – furniture was turned upside down, drawers were pulled out, clothes and jewellery were strewn around the place. The fridge had been raided, just as Raphael's had been, but other than that, it was hard to see what had been taken.

Pippa did not know what to think as she

carefully picked her way through the debris, following Dash.

When they came out into the garden again, Dash suddenly became extremely animated and went scooting off into the bushes at the far side of the lawn. He returned, ears flapping and tail wagging, carrying something in his jaws.

'What's the little fella got?' Raphael said, peering at Dash.

'Muffgfgfgule!' said Dash, jumping up excitedly.

Pippa bent down and took the item from Dash's mouth. It was something black and white; a bit soggy and crumpled, but it was otherwise one hundred per cent immediately recognizable as . . .

'Minx's scarf!' Pippa cried.

'She must have been here,' Dash said. 'Maybe we have been barking up the wrong tree.'

Pippa groaned. 'No time for bad jokes, Dash.'

'I wasn't joking,' the little dog protested. 'What

197

if Minx is the burglar and the dog isn't anything to
do with this?'

Raphael's features darkened. 'No! That lovely
little miss could never be a burglar,' he said loyally.

'Anyway – I don't understand. You said you had
picked up de scent! You said it was the Dalmatian
everybody has been seein' in the town,' he
blustered.

'I *had* picked up *a* scent,' said Dash, 'and I still
think the Dalmatian has been here. But the scarf

 **198**

most definitely is Minx's,' he insisted. 'And the question has to be asked: what was Minx doing in Marble's garden?'

As if on cue, Marble appeared at the garden gate. 'I don't believe it!' she cried. 'The intruder has been through my neighbour's garden too! The fence is broken and there's mayhem all down the street! Poor Snooksie is so terrified he won't come out.'

Pippa, still clutching Minx's scarf, hopped on to her skateboard and tore through the gate with Raphael close behind. Dash ran ahead, nose to the ground. They ran through the gardens, Dash hot on the trail. Each lawn they zipped across had been scuffed up and scratched at, each fence had been toppled or crashed through. It was tough going on a skateboard, so Pippa had to give up and tuck it under her arm again as she ran. (Fortunately for her she was as strong as she was fearless – remember I told you about the time she went creeping out of her house after dark to do some spying?)

Flowers had been squashed, bushes had holes in,
little fruit trees were swaying dangerously, clothes
had been pulled from washing lines and flung
around in a wild, frenzied fashion, decorating trees
and shrubs with the neighbourhood's pants and
socks.

Pippa couldn't help thinking how funny it
looked, in spite of the chaos. An underwear tree! she
sniggered to herself.

'We must be getting closer,' Dash panted. 'The
scent is getting stronger and the trail is fresher.'

They raced through six or seven gardens, but as
they approached the next, Dash stopped abruptly,
his ears alert, his nose in the air. Pippa ran into him
and Raphael toppled into the back of her.

'Shh!' Dash hissed, cocking one ear in the
direction of the next garden, which was enclosed
by a high hedge. There was a hole in this hedge too
and Dash seemed particularly interested in it. He
padded silently up to the gap in the greenery and

sniffed vigorously at it, then went up on to the tips of his paws and craned his neck to see. Tilting his head to indicate his friends should follow quietly after, he leaped daintily through the opening.

Pippa and Raphael climbed through, their hearts thudding in their throats. They stood next to Dash and stared at the sight before them, hardly daring to breathe.

There, sitting in the middle of the lawn, panting heavily, its long pink tongue lolling out of the side of its wide-open mouth, was an extremely large, long-legged white dog covered in black spots. Its eyes were big and shining as though dazed by the chaos left in its wake, and its huge paws were covered in mud and clumps of grass and leaves. But most bizarre of all was what it was wearing slung about its body.

'That's Minx's bag!' Pippa said out of the corner of her mouth.

'And look at the collar,' said Dash.

Raphael squinted. 'It – it be exactly like de

necklace she wear,' he whispered.

Pippa nodded. 'And it's got the tag on that we found in the bag, Dash – look!'

Dash crouched down to the floor and hissed to Pippa to stand back.

'What are you doing?' she muttered. 'Lying down for a snooze isn't going to achieve anything. We need to grab the animal before it hares off and causes more havoc!'

'I am showing the dog that I mean no harm,' said Dash through gritted teeth. 'And if you would only shut up I can focus on the matter in hand.'

Raphael put a hand on Pippa's arm to restrain her. She rolled her eyes, but did as she was told.

'Now listen to me,' Dash was saying to the Dalmatian in a measured tone. 'I am sure you've been through hell today. So have I, as a matter of fact—'

'Da-ash!' Pippa protested.

The dachshund gave an irritable flick of his tail and continued talking to the Dalmatian. 'I'm not

 **202**

going to hurt you. I mean, look at me! I'm under half your size. So why don't you tell me what's been going on and then Pippa and I can help you.'

The Dalmatian cowered and Pippa saw that the poor thing was shaking. Honestly, that Minx has got a lot to answer for, she thought.

Suddenly the Dalmatian let out an almighty wail, lifting its head to the skies and howling like a wolf. Raphael was the one who was shivering and shaking now.

'D-D-D-ash,' he said through chattering teeth. 'I tink we should get out of—'

But he didn't have time to finish his sentence because it was the Dalmatian who decided to make the first move. It shot the friends a wild look and then with a final, desperate YOOOWWL, it took off over the next fence.

'Quick! Follow that dog!' shouted Pippa, and leaped after the spotty pooch.

Dash jumped into Raphael's arms and the two of

them were soon in hot pursuit as well.

The fence belonged to the last of the long line
of houses and as soon as the trio were over it they
realized they were on the outskirts of Crumbly-
under-Edge and in open countryside. A beautiful
view of rolling green hills and patchwork fields
and hedges stretched ahead of them for miles. As
well as being a lovely sight, the lack of gardens and

hedges certainly made the going easier for them. Unfortunately it made the going easier for the Dalmatian as well.

Neither Pippa on her skateboard, nor Dash on his speedy little legs, nor Raphael on his rollerblades had a hope in heaven of catching up with the dynamo dog ahead of them. In fact, within minutes, the Dalmatian was so far ahead that it was difficult to make it out in detail. So difficult that when Dash said, 'Hang on a sec! I could swear that dotty dog is wearing an orange hat – where did that come from?' Raphael just laughed and told him he was 'seeing things, man!'

But Pippa had stopped trying to keep up and was staring after the crazy canine. Dash was right, it was wearing something orange on its head. And now its legs had changed from spotty all over to black all over. Maybe it's just mud, she told herself.

But when the dog seemed to get up on its hind legs and gradually become black from top to toe . . . and when it slung the Big Silver Bag purposefully

over its shoulder . . . and when it scratched its
right ear in a manner *everyone* recognized . . . and
then when it turned and waved at them before
disappearing over the hill . . .

'Well, goodness to mercy me!' cried Raphael, stopping in his tracks as well and staring ahead of him. 'Am I seein' tings too?' He whirled round and looked at Pippa and Dash.

No one knew what to say. It seemed as though the Dalmatian had turned into Minx before their disbelieving eyes.

The Bit at the End Where
Everything Is Sorted Out

Minx never did come back to Chop 'n' Chat to
explain herself. But luckily for Pippa, Raphael
and Dash she did write a letter, otherwise I doubt
anyone in Crumbly-under-Edge would have
believed what the friends had seen. Even Mrs Fudge
had her doubts when they had told her.

'People don't turn into dogs, dears,' she had said
gently. 'I think you must have been mistaken.'

But when Raphael arrived the next day waving
an envelope in his hand and smiling shakily, Mrs
Fudge knew she had to give them the benefit of the
doubt.

'I has an important bit of post for you today,
darlin'!' he cried, slamming the envelope down on

 208

the kitchen
work surface.

Mrs Fudge
took off her half-
moon spectacles
and cleaned them
on the edge of her

apron. The letter was decorated with black spots
and on the back it said: 'Sender: Ms Minx Polka'.

The little old lady sighed and sat down. 'I think
I need an extra-strong cup of tea before I read this,'
she said to Pippa.

'No problem, Mrs Fudge. I'll grab some lemony
biscuits too, in case you need sugar for shock. They
always say that sugar is good for shock and we
don't want you suffering from shock now, do we,
otherwise—'

'Yes, dear,' Mrs Fudge cut in on her babbling.

Pippa hurriedly made the tea and handed round
the biscuits. Raphael was so agitated he couldn't sit
down. Instead he drank his tea while circling the

kitchen on his rollerblades. Even Dash was fidgety and couldn't get comfy in his basket by the stove.

'Please, everyone! You're playing havoc with my nerves,' said poor Mrs Fudge. 'Sit still and I will read the letter out.'

So they did. And she did. And this is what it said:

Dear Mrs Fudge and Pippa and Dash and Raphael and Muffles (even though I know you didn't like me)

Raaaoooooow!!!
Well, you didn't, Muffles. There's no use in denying it.

'Someone tell that feline to put a sock in it!' Dash complained. 'Go on, Mrs Fudge, do.'

Mrs Fudge cleared her throat and read out the rest of the letter:

I am sorry. I am sorry for not coming back to explain myself. I am sorry for not telling you the truth. I am sorry for all the mess and upset I have caused. Because yes, your eyes weren't playing tricks on you today. I _did_ change into a Dalmatian and I _was_ the one who ran through everyone's houses and gardens and who frightened dogs in the park.

There's no easy way of writing this: I am a were-dog. When I was younger it was all right because it only happened at the full moon, so I could hide away until I was a girl again. But as I've got older, it's started happening more and more often. I went travelling to escape and I kept on the move for a couple of years so that no one would find out. But it was lonely and I wanted to come home.

I met this amazing guy on my travels – the dog whisperer I told you about (that bit was true) and I told him. He said that the reason I was changing into a Dalmatian more and more often was that

I was restless. Dalmatians are very restless dogs, you see. They need loads and loads of exercise and attention. The dog whisperer said that I would have to find a job to keep me busy – something really hectic that meant I had to be on my feet all day. That way, he said, I would wear myself out, and the Dalmatian part of me wouldn't come out so often. (He also gave me a recipe for those yummy biscuits, Dash. They were supposed to calm me down. They didn't work on me, but I found a good use for them, didn't I?)

Anyway, that's why I came to Chop 'n' Chat. And it sorted me out to start with, because I did work hard and it was tiring, so I stopped becoming a Dalmatian in the day and only changed at night. But then, I don't know what happened – maybe being around dogs all day affected me, or maybe I just wasn't getting enough sleep – anyhow, I started changing in the day again.

That last time was the worst. I couldn't control myself! Well, you saw what happened. And so

did the rest of Crumbly-under-Edge.

But don't worry. You won't see me again. I am going back to travelling. I'm going to find the dog whisperer again and see if he can help me once and for all.

Thanks for all the fun at Chop 'n' Chat. It's a great place to work. I am sad to say goodbye. I'll miss you. All of you – yes, you too, Pippa.

Love

Minx 'Dotty' Polka

xxx

Mrs Fudge put down the letter and shook her head in astonishment. 'But, I don't understand. How can a person *be* a dog?'

'It explains why she understood us all so well,' said Dash.

'And I has heard o' werewolves,' said Raphael, 'so I guess a were-dog isn't sooooo crazy.'

Pippa wanted to say that it was a load of rubbish,

that it was only Minx attention-seeking again, that things like were-dogs only existed in fairy tales. But she had seen the transformation for herself. So, for once, she didn't say a thing.

Dash raised a doggy eyebrow at her. 'Well, you know what they say: "Fact is stranger than fiction."'

Raphael sighed sadly. 'I will miss de girl, you know,' he said, looking at his feet.

'You're not the only one, dear,' said Mrs Fudge.

Pippa coughed. 'You haven't forgotten about me, have you, Mrs Fudge?'

The old lady smiled. 'Of course not.'

'Only, I haven't been allowed to do much in the salon recently – just make the tea and that, so could I *please* be allowed to do some clippety-clipping again?' Pippa pleaded.

'For pity's sake, let her,' said Dash. 'If only to shut her up.'

Mrs Fudge burst out laughing. 'All right,' she said. 'After all, what would I do without you, Pippa Peppercorn?'

This story was written by a lady called **Anna Wilson**. She lives in a town which is rather like Crumbly-under-Edge, where there is a hair salon a bit like Mrs Fudge's: the ladies there are just as lovely as Mrs Fudge (although not as old) and they love to eat cake. **Anna** has two cats, Jet and Inky, who are quite like Muffles (except they are black), and a pooch called Kenna (who doesn't actually like being pampered, unless it involves food). She also has three chickens who lay eggs that are perfect for cake-baking. Titch, one of the chickens, quite likes being pampered. **Anna** is thinking of setting up a Poultry Pampering Parlour just for her.

If you would like to find out more about **Anna** and her books you can visit www.annawilson.co.uk. Or you can write to her:

Anna Wilson
c/o Macmillan Children's Books
20 New Wharf Road
London
N1 9RR

Anna would love to see your pet photos too! But don't forget to enclose a stamped addressed envelope if you want her to return them to you.

Anna Wilson

**Welcome to the Pooch Parlour,
where mystery-solving has become
this season's hottest new look!**

Something very strange is going on in the cosy
village of Crumbly-under-Edge! Join Pooch Parlour
regulars Dash the dachshund and his human
friend Pippa 'chat-till-the-cows-come-home'
Peppercorn as they uncover a dastardly plot
involving oodles of snooty poodles . . .

Turn the page to read an extract

The Introductory Bit

This is the story of a small (and rather handsome) dog.

That'll be me she's talking about.

Yes. You don't need to be *quite* so conceited though, do you?

Sorry about that. As I was saying. This is the story of a small dog and how he solved a large (and rather tricky) mystery. His name is – no, I shan't tell you his name yet. That would spoil things, and we can't have that. You'll have to read on to find out what his name is, as he doesn't appear until later. I can, however, tell you the name of the lovely lady he came to live with, because she is in this story right from the beginning, so that won't spoil anything at all. Now you'd better stop fidgeting, because we're ready to begin.

Welcome to Crumbly-under-Edge!

Mrs Fudge was the lovely old lady in question. She had snowy-white hair and a jolly face and her full name was Semolina Ribena Fudge, which I'm sure you'll agree is quite an awkward name, and it's true that she wasn't overly fond of it. She didn't mind the 'Fudge' bit as that had been her late husband's surname. (I say he was her 'late husband', not because he was never on time for anything, but because, sadly, he was dead by the time this story starts.)

He was a wonderful man, dears (if a little bossy at times).

Mr and Mrs Fudge had travelled the world together – and the Seven Seas. They'd fought pirates and swum with dolphins. But after many years of adventure they decided it was time to settle down. And that is how they came to buy their large, rambling house in Liquorice Drive in the country town of Crumbly-under-Edge.

Crumbly-under-Edge was a sleepy, pretty little place. It had a main street with a few shops. And it had some windy, cobbledy not-so-main streets with houses painted pleasing shades of blue and pink and green and creamy white so that, from a distance, they looked like rows of marshmallows or iced buns. The houses and shops were very well looked after.

By the time you come to meet her, dear reader, Mrs Fudge had been living in the town for years and years and eons and indeed yonks (which is a technical term for a very long time indeed). She was quite happy – however she did feel the house was rather too big for one old person. And never having approved of waste of any kind (especially a waste of space), Mrs Fudge thought *maybe* she should open up part of her house for the purposes of running a little business. So, after much thought and planning, she came up with the idea of turning part of the ground floor of the house into a hairdressing salon called 'Chop 'n' Chat'.

There's always ladies wanting their hair done.

And how right she was about that! Chop 'n' Chat was soon a *booming* business, for not only was Mrs Fudge a marvellous hairdresser, she was also a very good listener and made the best cup of tea and the lightest fluffiest sponge cake this side of the Atlantic Ocean (I can't speak for the other side, not having been there myself at the time of writing).

So Mrs Fudge had arranged her life so that it

was just about perfect, you might say . . . There was one thing though: even though Mrs Fudge had many, many customers who kept her busy, and even though she had a particularly gorgeous fluffy grey cat called Muffles, and even though she *loved* her town and her house and her baking, Mrs Fudge could get lonely sometimes.

And this was a thought that kept her up at night occasionally and made the long winter evenings seem even longer and more wintery than they actually were. It became clear to Mrs Fudge that she had to do something about this. And so she pondered . . .

And that's where I come in.

Yes, thank you, Pippa . . . (It would be nice if people didn't *insist* on interrupting me.)

Pippa Peppercorn was a girl (obviously) who was ten and a quarter, and didn't mind who knew it. In fact, she was exceedingly proud of the quartery bit, as it meant she was well on her way to becoming eleven (which is, as everyone knows, almost fully grown-up). She had very few friends her own age, mainly because she felt that most other ten-and-a-quarter-year-olds were only interested in sleepover parties and giggling, whereas *she* had her eye firmly fixed on the future.

And, as it happened, Mrs Fudge was of the opinion that most other extremely old people were rather dull and only liked sucking toffees and saying, 'It wouldn't happen in my day.' So when Pippa walked into Chop 'n' Chat one day with a sulk that could have sunk a thousand ships and muttered, 'Teacher says I have to get my hair cut,' and Mrs Fudge smiled in an understanding way and said, 'Would you like an apricot flapjack?' a lifelong friendship was born.

Now we've got all that straight, I think we should get on with the story.

What about me?
I've already explained:
you come in later.
But—
I've got to set the scene, haven't I?
But—!
Who's telling this story?
sulks

8

2

Pippa Peppercorn Comes to the Rescue

In the usual run of things, you would expect that a girl of ten and a quarter would have to ask her parents' permission to take on a Saturday job. But luckily for Pippa (and for this story) we don't have to worry about all that. Pippa's parents were always busy, and when they heard that the wonderful Mrs Fudge was giving their daughter something to do at the weekend they were so over the moon that they could have written to the Association of Astronauts to tell them what the dark side of it looked like. (Dark, presumably.)

'That is a lovely idea,' said Mr Peppercorn, not looking up from his newspaper.

'Make sure Mrs Fudge gives you the recipe for her

sponge cake, won't you?' said Mrs Peppercorn, not
looking up from her book.

And you won't hear much more from Pippa
Peppercorn's parents, because frankly they were such
a tedious pair it would bore you rigid.

Pippa found herself counting down the days,
hours, minutes and seconds until that first Saturday
morning arrived. And since counting every second
of every day takes rather a lot of concentration Pippa
missed out on a few things, such as people asking her

to partner them for table tennis or go to the cinema with them. But Pippa didn't notice. She was too busy counting.

The Saturday of Pippa's new job finally dawned. But Pippa was up well before the dawn. She was up while it was as dark as the darkest cave. And to top it all, her bedside light wasn't working, so she fell out of bed and had to fumble around for her slippers and a torch, which luckily she always kept under the bed in case of burglars. She thought that if a burglar was ever cheeky enough to come into her room in the dark, she could grab her torch, shine it in his face to bedazzle the daylights out of him and then make a run for it.

She found the torch, turned it on and got dressed. Then she crept downstairs and made herself some pancakes and fried some bacon and boiled the kettle for a cup of tea. Pippa was quite handy like that.

But even after she'd done all those things, the kitchen clock insisted that it was only seven o'clock.

'Oh, blow it!' Pippa told the clock. 'Couldn't you

11

please move a little bit faster? I'm going to have to give the kitchen a good old clean now to pass the time.'

The clock unfortunately did not react to being told off, even when Pippa gave it her hardest glare, so she put her hands on her skinny hips, sighed a big loud snorty sigh and looked around her to decide where to start on her cleaning.

The kitchen was not very dirty or messy, so she decided to pass the time by rearranging things instead of cleaning them. She became so absorbed in moving chairs and jugs and plates and bowls and pots and pans that, without her noticing, the kitchen clock eventually *did* get a move on and all of a sudden (or so it seemed), it was . . .

'HALF PAST EIGHT!' Pippa shouted, punching the air in a victory salute, narrowly missing the rather beautiful pyramid she had made of all the cups and saucers in the house.

She ran to the hall, took her red duffel coat from its peg, grabbed her black woolly hat and, checking

 12

she had her keys, let herself out into the cold autumn morning.

Mrs Fudge too was awake before the dawn had leaked around the edges of the sky. She found that the older she got, the less sleep she tended to need, and so she was often up at a time most normal people would be cosily tucked up in bed. This meant that she had lots of extra time in her day for doing all the things she had been too busy to do when she was younger, namely baking, learning the banjo and knitting. (Sometimes she even knitted little cakes to use as cheery decorations.)

And so, even though it was incredibly early and still rather dark outside, Mrs Fudge was up and about. She had neatly brushed and combed her hair, and she was wearing a fresh dress (her favourite one, with the red and pink swirls) with a blue flowery apron over it to keep herself clean. She was humming a little song of her own devising and tidying her kitchen and baking some scones. The wind howled outside, sending flurries of leaves leaping and whirling against the windows, but Mrs Fudge's kitchen was invitingly snug and warm.

'I must make the place look extra-specially cosy and nice for young Pippa's first day,' she said, as she shined the taps on the sink.

She wasn't talking to herself, I should add. She was talking to her cat, Muffles. Muffles wasn't paying

 14

attention though. She was licking her bottom, as cats have a habit of doing when you are talking to them. It's rude and ungracious of them, I agree, but what can you do? A cat will always lick its bottom if it possibly can.

which is why DOGS are so much more sophisticated.

Mrs Fudge tutted (as indeed I will do to a CERTAIN DOG in a minute), sighed and went back to tidying the kitchen until the timer went PING! which meant the scones were ready. She fetched a stripy oven glove and bent to open the oven door. As she did so, a warm, golden crumbly smell of good fresh baking filled the room. Mrs Fudge closed her eyes, the better to appreciate the aroma, and smiled.

'Enough for all my customers this morning,' she said appreciatively, opening her eyes again and setting the scones down on a wire rack to cool.

The sun was peeking in through the crack in the curtains by now, the wind had calmed its bad temper and the kettle had just boiled. Muffles opened one eye to check that everything was as it should be, saw that it was, and closed it again. Mrs Fudge made herself a nice pot of tea and sank down into her favourite armchair by the window to have five minutes' peace before her day began.